THE SNARK WAS A BOOJUM

When William Baker is found dead, his naked and twisted body lying under a bench in the dingy waiting room of a train station, the village police are baffled. Soon afterward another corpse appears, this time posthumously stuffed into full evening dress, with black pigment smeared on his face. A murderer is at large whose M.O. is to use his victims to recreate scenes from Lewis Carroll's nonsense poem, 'The Hunting of the Snark' — and it's up to amateur detective Simon Gale to stop him before he kills again.

GERALD VERNER
and CHRIS VERNER

---◆---

THE SNARK
WAS A
BOOJUM

Complete and Unabridged

LINFORD
Leicester

First published in Great Britain

First Linford Edition
published 2017

A catalogue record for this book is available
from the British Library.

ISBN 978–1–4448–3421–5

Published by
F. A. Thorpe (Publishing)
Anstey, Leicestershire

Set by Words & Graphics Ltd.
Anstey, Leicestershire
Printed and bound in Great Britain by
T. J. International Ltd., Padstow, Cornwall

This book is printed on acid-free paper

Posthumous Dedication
For my daughter-in-law Jenny
and for Mark and Zoe,
my grandchildren I never met.

'It's a Snark!' was the sound that
   first came to their ears,
And seemed almost too good to
   be true.
Then followed a torrent of
   laughter and cheers:
Then the ominous words 'It's a
   Boo — '

Then, silence. Some fancied they
   heard in the air
A weary and wandering sigh
That sounded like ' — jum!' but
   the others declare
It was only a breeze that went
   by.

They hunted till darkness came
   on, but they found
Not a button, or feather, or
   mark,
By which they could tell that they
   stood on the ground
Where the Baker had met with
   the Snark.

In the midst of the word he was
    trying to say,
In the midst of his laughter and
    glee,
He had softly and suddenly
    vanished away —
For the Snark *was* a Boojum,
    you see.

'The Hunting of the Snark'
by Lewis Carroll

PART ONE

The Vanishing

They hunted till darkness came
    on, but they found
Not a button, or feather, or
    mark,
By which they could tell that they
    stood on the ground
Where the Baker had met with
    the Snark.

'The Hunting of the Snark'
by Lewis Carroll

1

I realised, afterwards, that murder must have been in the mind of the murderer long before the dinner party at Hunter's Meadow.

There is no doubt that murder would have been committed in any event, but it is almost equally certain that it would not have taken the grotesque and horrible form it did if Simon Gale, in that joking reference concerning the people at the dinner-table, had not supplied the murderer with a plan.

The long dining room, in deep shadow except for the soft light from the candles in the two silver candelabra at each end of the refectory table, with the servants moving silently like ghosts, is a memory that lingered vividly in my mind long after the whole, grim business was over. It was like the last glimpse of a sane well-ordered community before the thin crust cracked open to let out some of the strange and terrifying things that writhed beneath.

It is curious how an apparently trivial incident can mushroom out into something that changes your entire life. I should never have got mixed up in this hideous business, at first hand, anyway, if my father had not left his umbrella behind at the office. The severe chill, which resulted from him getting soaked to the skin on his way home, laid him up in bed with a steadily mounting temperature and an equally mounting temper when he should have been staying at Hunter's Meadow as the guest of Joshua Bellman. The consequence was that as the only available representative of that ancient and highly respected firm of solicitors, Trueman, Hartly, Ward and Trueman, I had to go to Lower Bramsham in his place.

There was nobody else. There has not been a Hartly or a Ward in the firm for over ninety years. Nowadays it consists of only my father and myself and old Timothy Wyse, our managing clerk, who probably knows more about law than either of us — certainly more than I do.

'You'll *have* to go, Jeff,' croaked my father irritably from among his rumpled pillows. 'Bellman's our most important client. He wants to talk over the legal details of this new acquisition.'

And that's how I came to be at the dinner party on that Friday evening, and involved, at the very beginning, in this strange affair that began as a joke and ended so horribly in the locked hut in the wood near Farley Halt.

It was a warm night in late September, and the windows of the long dining room were open with the curtains undrawn, but the air was so still that the candle flames on the table scarcely wavered. An unexpected spell of fine weather had succeeded the cold and the rain of the previous weeks and looked like lasting for a few more days at least. There was a nearly full moon, and the wide terrace outside the windows, with its stone urns of dying flowers, looked spectral in the bluish-white light; like the backcloth in a theatre or an illustration from a book of fairy-tales. You could almost imagine that

5

people of a bygone and more gracious age moved silently over the old flagstones. It was easy in this ancient house, which had seen Henry Tudor on the English throne, to imagine ghosts.

There were, including myself, thirteen of us grouped round the heavy carved-oak table that evening. With the exception of Joshua Bellman, whom I had met once or twice at our London office, I knew none of them. From what I had gathered, during a rather sketchy introduction over cocktails in the drawing room, they were mostly local people. Taking advantage of a story that had something to do with a deal in shares, which threatened to be both dull and interminable, I tried to sort out what little I knew about them. The story was being related with a great deal of throaty enjoyment by a stout red-faced man sitting almost opposite me. The stout man's name was Arnold Hope, I remembered, and the dark, rather pretty woman in the vivid scarlet dress next to him was a Mrs. Hilary King, who designed hats for a London firm of milliners. The big square-faced man with the heavy jowls and sonorous voice was a barrister. Now, what was his name? Cranston, that was it. Edward Cranston.

' . . . these shares continued to fall, but I was convinced they would recover. The time element was the difficulty. Settling day was barely a week ahead.' The strangled voice of Mr. Hope droned huskily on in the background. Ignoring it, I transferred my attention from the impressive figure of Edward Cranston to the delicate and wholly charming one of the woman on his left. Although she must have been in her late sixties, there was scarcely a discernible line in her placid and gentle face. Miss Agnes Beaver looked as though life had been a very happy and tranquil adventure. Except that her faded grey eyes held a hint of sadness.

That brought me to the last person on that side of the table: a dark-haired, good-looking man with a rather supercilious curl to his short upper lip. I had no difficulty in placing him. In the first few seconds of our acquaintance, Lance Weston had informed me that he wrote novels; had already published three, and was halfway through a fourth; that they sold extremely well, and what did I think of them? Since I hadn't read any of them, I couldn't tell him. There was something so intensely vital about him that I felt that any length of time spent in his company would leave me completely drained. He sucked away your energy with the competence of a vacuum cleaner sucking up dust.

On his left, at the foot of the table and facing her husband at the head, but almost entirely screened from him by the massive arms of a silver candelabra, sat my hostess, Ursula Bellman. Candlelight is flattering to most women, but Ursula Bellman would have been beautiful in any light. She was fair, with that very pale gold hair that looks almost silver; and her eyes, beneath fine-drawn, curving brows, were a deep, nearly violet, blue. She wore, so that her arms and shoulders were the whiter by contrast, a plain dress of black velvet, cut low, with a single diamond clip at the breast. A beautiful woman who was well aware of her beauty.

I glanced at the head of the table where Joshua Bellman sat, his thin blue-veined and predatory hands busily peeling a peach, and wondered what had induced a woman like Ursula to marry such a dried-up-looking little man. The answer was probably money. Bellman's chain stores had branches in many towns throughout the British Isles, and new ones were opening in the United States. He also controlled a number of subsidiary companies specialising in baking, breakfast cereals, pies, wholesale supplies, and dairy products. Bellman was a very wealthy man. But even with that inducement . . . ? With a slight shock, I discovered that he had raised his small shrewd brown eyes and was watching me. I had a disconcerting feeling that he knew what I was thinking, and rather hastily I looked away.

Wedged in between an enormously fat woman who bulged wherever it was possible to bulge out of a hideous dress of a particularly revolting shade of puce, and a very dapper man with grey hair, was a small sandy-haired individual whose name I could not for the life of me remember. He was staring down at his plate and fiddling nervously with his knives, forks and spoons, so that he kept up a continuous muted tinkling, like the distant sound of sleighbells, to the intense irritation of the grey-haired man next to him. This man had been introduced to me as Franklin Gifford, the manager of the local bank — fastidious and possessing a certain charm, but with a hint of cruelty in his eyes.

Arnold Hope's apparently endless negotiations with the shares, which by now had become so involved that it was quite impossible to follow them at all, went on relentlessly. Only two more people remained to complete my list — Jack Merridew, Bellman's lantern-jawed secretary, whose large shell-rimmed spectacles gave him an appearance of owlish wisdom; and an extraordinary-looking man who occupied the place of honour on his host's right. His unruly hair was the rich colour of a ripe horse-chestnut, and he was the possessor of a bristling and belligerent beard of the same lurid hue. Earlier in the evening his booming voice, which matched his large bulk, had dominated the table, but this was some time before Arnold Hope had begun his pointless story of the complex share deal. He had fallen into a glowering silence, twining his restless fingers in his beard and staring at his plate with an expression of the most fiendish malignancy that I have ever seen on a human face. Except that his name was Simon Gale, and that he appeared to be someone of importance, I know nothing about him, but he definitely had a most remarkable personality — and not one that I particularly liked.

Later, I was to change this first impression.

Although they had no premonition of it at the time, these were the people who were to become involved with murder in its most fantastic and terrible form. That's not quite true. As I afterwards learned, there was one person present who *certainly* had.

Arnold Hope's story at last came to an abrupt end; the shares had somehow sorted themselves out to his immense advantage. With a grunt, his red face shining, he looked round the table triumphantly. He said, with a note of challenge in that strangled voice: 'What do you think of that, eh? What do you think of that?'

I felt an almost irresistible desire to tell him, but the only words that would have described what I thought were barred in polite society, so I refrained.

Simon Gale growled something into his beard that ended in a suspicious sibilance, and Bellman gave him a quick sidelong look with an unexpected glint of humour in his small eyes. There was a swift unintelligible murmur from the others, whether of appreciation or relief I wasn't sure, and Lance Weston almost immediately began to relate an incident that he declared had happened to him during the war. It was a good story and he told it well. Even Bellman added a dry chuckle to the general laughter.

'I don't believe it for a moment,' asserted Mrs. King, shaking her dark head. 'Not for a moment!'

'I assure you,' protested Weston solemnly, 'that it's the absolute, unvarnished truth!'

'Would you be prepared to confirm that under oath?' asked Cranston heavily, as though dealing with a hostile witness.

The fat woman, whom I suddenly remembered was the wife of the boring Mr. Hope, bulged a little further out of the puce dress as she leaned forward. With a roguish look in her prominent and rather washed-out blue eyes, she said: 'It isn't fair, is it, Mr. Weston? I'm sure so *many* things happen that you'd never *believe* possible, yet you know they did. Sometimes the most peculiar things. You've only got to read the newspapers, haven't you? Only the other day, a man cut up all his wife's hats and threw them at the milkman!'

'I'd find it harder to believe,' boomed Simon Gale, 'if the man had cut up the milkman and thrown the pieces at his wife's hats!'

'Some of the hats I've seen,' said Mrs. King, with professional disparagement, 'deserve to be cut up! Ridiculous hats! Really awful!'

'Ursula was wearing one the other day,' grunted Bellman mischievously, 'that looked like a poached egg.'

Mrs. King gave him a venomous look. 'I designed that hat for your wife, Mr. Bellman.'

'He knows you did, Hilary,' said Ursula in her low and altogether captivating voice. 'He's teasing. Anyway, men have no idea what suits a woman.'

'Precious few women have either,' remarked Arnold Hope, eyeing his wife gloomily. 'Look dreadful, most of 'em.'

'Men are so ungrateful,' insisted Mrs. Hope to the table in general, oblivious that her husband's remark had any relevance to herself. 'We dress to please them and they seldom appreciate our efforts, do they?'

'The majority of women,' retorted Lance Weston, with the air of uttering an original and profound piece of wisdom, 'dress with one object — to provoke the envy of other women.'

'I really don't think that's true, Mr.

Weston,' put in little Miss Beaver in a gentle voice. 'It makes a woman feel better if she knows she's well dressed. It gives her confidence. Don't you agree?'

'You're absolutely right, Agnes,' agreed Ursula with a meaningful glance at her husband. 'Men really don't know much about us, do they?'

Bellman cut in with a remark deliberately intended to change the subject. The conversation became split up among little isolated groups. Lance Weston began talking to Gifford about the state of the local golf course, a hazard at the ninth hole — a discussion which, after listening for a moment or two in silence, Ursula joined in. They argued happily, with Ursula holding a kind of watching brief, until she got tired of the subject and started talking across them to Agnes Beaver.

Cranston, Hope, and Mrs. King began a three-sided discussion concerning a recent divorce case, which appeared to be chiefly notable for the fact that the outraged husband had cited no less than three co-respondents in a matter of six weeks. Considering that the wife in question was a woman of nearly sixty, this seemed to me to be pretty good going.

Mrs. Hope, to my dismay, singled me out for her special attention. She prattled merrily on about a number of quite uninteresting subjects, mostly connected with local events I knew nothing about. I listened patiently, secure in the knowledge it was quite unnecessary to answer.

It was in the midst of all this that Simon Gale dropped his bombshell. There was a slight lull for a second in the chatter going round the table. In the silence, Ursula's voice, soft but with clarity, could be heard addressing part of a sentence to Miss Beaver. ' . . . yards of lovely lace. I do think you're so clever to make lace like that.'

That did it! There was a sudden and startling crash as Simon Gale brought his fist down on the table beside his plate. The flames of the candles wavered. The glass and china rattled and rang. 'By all the bulls of the Borgias,' he roared, his beard quivering excitedly, 'I've got it!'

There was an awful and complete

silence. Mrs. Hope gave such a frightened jump that she nearly came completely out of her puce dress. Twelve outraged and astonished faces turned towards the perpetrator of this unexpected and wholly reprehensible interruption.

'What exactly is it that you've got?' asked Mrs. Hope, swallowing.

Gale appeared unmoved by the sensation he had caused. Judging by the gleam in his eye, I think he was enjoying himself.

'It's been worrying me all evening, d'you see?' he told them. 'I couldn't make out what all you people reminded me of.'

Mrs. Hilary King eyed him without friendliness. She said caustically: 'Really? What is it we remind you of, Mr. Gale?'

'It was the lace that triggered it,' he explained, looking at Ursula. 'The lace, linking with Beaver and the rest.'

Arnold Hope ran a podgy hand over his thinning hair. His eyes, small and astonished, stared in bewilderment. 'I don't understand. What are you driving at?' he demanded.

A huge and delighted grin spread over

Simon Gale's face. He looked like an overgrown and cheeky schoolboy. 'You're not real,' he cried. 'None of you. You're all out of a book!' He rubbed his huge hands together gleefully, but his own obvious enjoyment was met with thinly disguised hostility. It was quite evident that nobody understood what he was talking about. For a wild moment I thought that he must have had too much to drink. Looking around, I was quite sure that was the general opinion.

'By the snores of the seven sleepers, you must see it. It's so obvious!' He leaned forward and stabbed at each of them in turn with a massive forefinger. 'There's you, Bellman; there's Miss Beaver, who makes lace; there's a Mrs. King, a maker of bonnets and hoods; there's Hope, a stockbroker — '

'Retired,' interrupted Mrs. Hope quickly, as if there was some stigma in not being retired.

'There's a banker and a barrister,' Gale continued passionately, ignoring the interruption. 'And finally — this makes it complete — a Baker!' He pointed to the

18

sandy-haired little man between Mrs. Hope and Gifford.

I suddenly remembered. Of course, that was his name — William Baker. Then it came to me. I saw what Gale was getting at. What an extraordinary coincidence! ''The Hunting of the Snark'!' I exclaimed.

Simon Gale gave a whoop of delight. 'You've seen it! Yes, that's it!' He couldn't restrain his enthusiasm. In a voice that thundered through the room he quoted: ''The crew was complete: it included a Boots — a Maker of Bonnets and Hoods — a Barrister brought to arrange their disputes — and a Broker to value their goods.'' He paused, frowning. 'How does it go on?' He ruffled his unruly shock of hair impatiently. 'Something about a Banker engaged at enormous expense.'

On the faces of those gathered around the table appeared a few feeble and polite smiles. 'Very amusing,' remarked Cranston ponderously. He echoed my own thoughts. 'What a remarkable coincidence.'

Lewis Carroll's nonsense poem was

19

coming back to me now. I'd learned it by heart as a boy for a school recital. I wracked my brain to remember it: '*Just the place for a Snark!*' *the Bellman cried, as he landed his crew with care; Supporting each man on the top of the tide by a finger entwined in his hair.* Gale was right, the analogy was remarkable. Another verse popped into my head: *There was also a Beaver that paced on the deck, or would sit making lace in the bow: And had often (the Bellman said) saved them from wreck, though none of the sailors knew how.* I smiled to myself at the humour. A Beaver who sat making lace in the bow — how extraordinary!

'We haven't a Boots or a Billard-marker,' Gale continued with his theme.

'Or a Butcher,' I added.

'Or a Snark,' remarked Lance Weston with a curl of the lip. 'Is there a Snark among us?'

For the first time since we had sat down to dinner, Merridew spoke. He said with a slight stammer: 'P-perhaps that's just as well. It wouldn't be good for Mr. Baker, would it?'

'Why?' asked Ursula, looking at him with a completely blank expression on her lovely face.

I already knew the answer. I watched in amusement the reactions of those in front of me. Merridew reddened slightly and touched his glasses.

'It-it might be a B-Boojum,' he answered with a nervous smile on his lips. 'Wasn't it the Baker's uncle who w-warned his nephew about the Snark being a Boojum?'

'You're dead right,' declared Gale with great gusto, waving his arms about, to the immediate danger of the glasses near his plate. ''But oh, beamish nephew, beware of the day, if your Snark be a Boojum! For then, you will softly and suddenly vanish away, and never be met with again!''

Outside on the terrace, there was a little scurry and rustle of dried leaves. The flames of the candles flickered and swayed. Ursula Bellman shivered in the sudden draught. Bellman saw it and turned sharply to Trenton, the butler, who was hovering in the shadows. 'Close

21

the windows,' he ordered curtly.

Cranston turned to the little sandy-haired man, who was looking rather bewildered. 'Better be careful, Baker,' he said facetiously, grasping the lapels of his dinner jacket as though it were a gown. 'Search your house thoroughly when you get home in case there should be a Boojum lurking about.' He gave a dry laugh.

Swiftly, but with a smooth and graceful movement, Ursula rose to her feet. 'Coffee will be in the drawing room,' she announced.

2

The dinner party, the details of which were to become etched on our minds, took place on the Friday. It was not until the following Monday that the incredible thing happened that turned the hitherto peaceful village of Lower Bramsham into a place where terror stalked the ancient streets, and people who had never bothered before locked their doors at night.

What had only existed in one person's warped mind as a vague and formless shape, like something half-seen emerging from a mist, had been brought into sharp and hideous focus by Simon Gale's allusion at the dinner party. The desire to kill, as we knew afterwards, had been present for a long time, but had lacked a coherent design until that moment.

The weather remained fine until the Monday afternoon, and I spent the greater part of the weekend in exploring the amenities of Lower Bramsham; Bellman having, rather to my relief, decided not to start work on the details of his merger until the beginning of the week.

Lower Bramsham proved to be nearly all Tudor, which means that it consisted of a great deal of old oak and whitewash. There was a fine old church and a charming high street that ran down to a white-railed green, round which clustered a number of cottages. Facing them was the Golden Crust.

The pub had started out as a bakery until around the beginning of the century, when an enterprising firm of brewers had converted the bakehouse into a saloon bar, retaining the original name. The barmaid, a buxom blonde with suspiciously golden hair, and glittering with fake jewellery like a crystal chandelier, exuded an exotic perfume from the deep recesses of her ample figure every time she moved. She went by the name of Beatrice Umble. In spite of an ultra-refined accent into which she occasionally introduced a completely unnecessary aspirate, she was warm-hearted, good-humoured, and immensely popular. She and Simon Gale became fast friends almost on sight.

Simon and I were the only guests staying at Hunter's Meadow, and in consequence we saw quite a lot of each other that weekend, and quite a lot of the Golden Crust. I've never known anybody who could down beer in such large quantities as Simon Gale. I got to know him quite well, and, in spite of all his bounce and bluster, not to mention other eccentricities, I liked him. He was completely uninhibited and had an enormous zest for life. Everything interested him. There was scarcely any subject that he didn't know something about and was prepared to discuss in the loud booming voice that was part of his vivid personality. What seemed at first to be affectation, I found upon knowing him better, was a natural characteristic of the man that he could no more help than the colour of his hair. His vanity was colossal. I'm convinced that he would have tackled anything in the world with the complete assurance that he could make a success of it.

I discovered to my surprise that in addition to being an artist of some repute, he was the inventor of the well-known breakfast cereal, Gale's Golden Flakes, and that it was through this asset that he first became acquainted with Joshua Bellman.

'When the stuff caught on,' he explained to me on one occasion when we were heading to the Golden Crust, 'orders were pouring in faster than we could cope with 'em, and I made the decision to get out while I was ahead and enjoy life a bit. So I leased the world manufacturing rights to Bellman for a thundering lump sum down an' a whacking big royalty. He tried to whittle me down, but I refused to accept a ha'penny less than I originally demanded. He's got great respect for me 'cause of that.' He chuckled delightedly.

I thought this must have been a considerable achievement. Joshua Bellman was noted as a driver of a hard bargain.

'Ever since then,' Gale went on, 'I've had a kind of standing invitation to come an' stay at Hunter's Meadow whenever I felt like it.'

I was glad that he had felt like it at that particular time. If it hadn't been for Gale and the Golden Crust, I should have found it pretty dull. Bellman spent most of that weekend shut up in his study, an austere room on the second floor furnished with the bare necessities of an office, and only put in an appearance at lunch and dinner. I didn't see much of Ursula, either. She was out a lot, playing golf with Lance Weston, Cranston and Mrs. King. I can't say I blamed her for wanting to get out of that house. There wasn't much fun to be had in Hunter's Meadow.

On the Monday morning, Gale and I had just finished breakfast. Ursula and old Joshua always had theirs sent up on trays to their respective rooms, so there were just the two of us chatting when Merridew came in with a message from Bellman that he'd like to see me in his study as soon as possible.

I left Gale deftly rolling one of his acrid cigarettes from the battered tin of strong black tobacco that he usually carried in his jacket pocket, and followed the secretary upstairs. Bellman was sitting at his desk with an open file in front of him, and for the rest of the morning we tackled the details of the acquisition, the purchase of a number of shops, two warehouses and a factory from a Mr. Benjamin Fisk. We kept at it, with a break for lunch, during the whole of the afternoon, but even by then we hadn't made very much headway. Bellman was as stubborn as a jammed window-frame, and argued over every clause, and I soon saw that it was going to take a long time before I came in sight of anything like a final draft and the end of my ordeal.

It had been raining steadily since midday from a sky of unbroken grey, but during the evening it cleared up a little. Ursula had a headache and dined in her room; and Bellman, who looked thoroughly exhausted and more dried-up than normal, muttered an excuse after the coffee was served, and left Gale and myself to our own devices.

Suddenly without warning, Gale leapt from his chair with an expression of exasperation. 'Come on, young feller,' he cried, his mind made up. 'We're going out.' He strode into the hall and struggled into a disreputable raincoat. 'Fresh air and beer, hey?'

It had been a depressing day, and I welcomed his suggestion with relief. A thin mist was rising from the sodden ground when we left Hunter's Meadow, but it had stopped actually raining, which was just as well because it was a good mile and a half walk to the Golden Crust.

Beatrice welcomed us with a smile as glittering as her jewellery. 'I was wondering if you two would be coming in,' she said, reaching for a pint tankard for Gale. 'Nicer in here than out there.'

Gale gave her a beaming smile. 'Neither wind nor rain, thunder or tempest, could keep me away from you!'

Beatrice loved this kind of banter. Coyly, from under mascara-laden eyelashes, she looked at Gale as she set a full and foaming tankard down on the bar.

'You men!' she exclaimed with a slight lift of one shoulder as she proceeded to fill a second tankard for me.

Simon Gale swallowed an enormous draught of beer and banged the tankard down on the bar. It was at that moment that the door opened and a woman came in, demanding my full attention. In spite of being a junior partner in an old established firm of solicitors, I've met quite a number of pretty women in my thirty-five years, and not all of them in a professional capacity. But this woman who had just entered the saloon bar struck me at once as being different. It wasn't that she was prettier. Actually, I suppose she wasn't pretty at all — but she had something about her that would have singled her out even among a Hollywood beauty chorus. She had a cute face and sex appeal in spades.

Her face was small and rather impish. At each corner of her large but nicely shaped mouth was a trace of a dimple that gave it the suggestion of a humorous quirk. Even the loose and fleecy coat she wore couldn't hide an admirable figure. I judged her to be in her late twenties.

She walked quietly over to the bar and spoke in a husky, attractive voice, asking for a whisky and ginger ale. I caught sight of Gale's quizzical grin and cocked eyebrow and realised I must have been staring at her like an idiot. Hastily I picked up my tankard and drank some beer to mask my embarrassment.

Beatrice was pushing a whisky and ginger across the bar towards the woman when she asked a totally unexpected question: 'I wonder if you could tell me the way to a place called Hunter's Meadow?'

Simon Gale swung round. 'Hunter's Meadow, hey?'

The woman turned her black and glossy head towards him. Her eyes, green under dark lashes, surveyed him coolly and appraisingly. 'Yes. I need to get there.'

'We're staying there,' Gale explained, waving one arm vaguely in my direction. 'If you're not in a desperate hurry to rush off, we can take you there, hey?'

She looked at him and then at me. Her face crinkled into a smile. 'That would be kind,' she answered. 'I'm not in a hurry. I have a car outside.'

'That's even better!' cried Gale. 'We can show you the way if you can give us a lift back. It's an infernally damp and muddy walk, d'you see? How's that, eh?'

Her smile widened and the dimples at the corners of her mouth deepened. She laughed. 'Just tell me when you're ready. My name's Zoe Anderson.'

'Mine's Simon Gale, an' this young feller is Jeff Trueman. He's a solicitor, but don't hold that against him — he can be quite intelligent. Hey, Beatrice!' he bellowed across the bar. 'We're thirsty! Same again!'

Beatrice was just completing our order when Lance Weston came in. He hesitated near the door, his eyes flickering swiftly round the bar.

'Hello, hello!' greeted Gale in a voice that made the bottle and glasses ring. 'Come on, Weston. You're just in time for Trueman's round. The more the merrier!'

Lance Weston approached us slowly. His face looked pale. He mumbled shakily: 'I could do with a drink — whisky.'

Gale looked at him sharply. 'Something wrong?'

'Wrong?' Weston uttered a dry laugh, thin and mirthless. He gave a slight nod. 'You won't believe it.'

There was an expression behind his eyes that puzzled me. He looked shocked, as if he'd just avoided a bad accident. He had our undivided attention as we stared at him curiously.

'What's happened is impossible,' he said.

Zoe Anderson fumbled in the pocket of her fleecy coat and took out a packet of cigarettes. Her green eyes were wide with the expectancy of some sort of revelation. She pulled a cigarette from the half-filled packet and twiddled it about in her fingers, staring from Lance Weston to us and back again.

'Don't talk in riddles,' bellowed Gale.

Weston looked at him accusingly. 'It's your fault,' he said. 'Those people and 'The Hunting of the Snark'.'

'What about it?' snapped Gale.

'William Baker.' Lance Weston's voice was hard and brittle. 'Your Snark was a Boojum right enough, Gale. Baker's vanished — literally into thin air! He walked out of his house at a quarter past nine and disappeared.'

'Nonsense!' cried Gale impatiently. 'He must've gone somewhere.'

'Without his clothes?' demanded Weston belligerently.

The atmosphere in the pub had become tense. I had a sense of foreboding. I saw a curious expression come into Gale's eyes. It was compounded of incredulity, uneasiness, and something else. In a voice totally unlike his bull roar, he asked: 'What do you mean, without his clothes?'

Beatrice, avid with curiosity, placed a whisky on the bar.

'They're all that's left of him,' answered Lance Weston, grabbing his whisky and downing it in one. 'The clothes he was wearing. Just a heap of clothes lying on the pavement where he disappeared.'

3

It was late that night before I learned the full details of the vanishing of William Baker. They only served to make his sudden disappearance more inexplicable.

Nothing would satisfy Simon Gale, after he heard what had happened, except the fullest information at first hand. He found out from Beatrice at the pub, who was a fountain of knowledge concerning most things that were going on in the local community, that Baker had lodgings with a Mrs. Tickford in Goose Lane, the entrance to which faced the Golden Crust on the other side of the green.

'We must go there at once,' boomed Gale, making for the door.

I could see that Zoe Anderson was bemused by all this, and I suggested I should accompany her back to Hunter's Meadow; but she wouldn't hear of it, insisting on driving us to Goose Lane. Gale was delighted at this offer, bubbling over with an intense and feverish curiosity that he was determined to satisfy without delay. We left Lance Weston, who refused to come with us, downing whiskies in the saloon bar.

* * *

Goose Lane turned out to be L-shaped and semi-rural. One end of it, the longer arm, was shut off by a high wall of brick that formed part of some farm buildings, and there was no outlet at all this way. The other and shorter arm came out on the green within a few yards of the cottage in which Lance Weston lived.

There were only four houses in Goose Lane, and these had been built on the left-hand side, almost under the high brick wall that shut off the farm buildings at the upper end. Below these four houses, which were small and more modern than the rest of Lower Bram-sham, was a high wattle fence that continued in an unbroken line until it joined the tarred fence surrounding the garden of Lance Weston's cottage. On the opposite side of the lane, and running down from the brick wall to the green, was a thick hedge that enclosed farmland.

Mrs. Tickford's house was the first of these four. When we arrived, Mrs. Tickford herself, a gaunt woman with a high, thin and distinctly unpleasant voice, was standing at her garden gate, discussing with her immediate neighbours the extraordinary and altogether inexplicable disappearance of her lodger.

There was no difficulty in getting them to tell us what had happened. William Baker's disappearance had made such a powerful impression on them that they were only too eager to go on repeating the story until someone told them to stop.

William Baker occupied the upstairs front room in Mrs. Tickford's house as a bed-sitting room. He had his own latchkey to the front door, and, except for his breakfast, which was served in his room on a tray, had all his meals out. He had been living there for the past three weeks, and according to Mrs. Tickford had proved an exemplary lodger in every way, which meant that she hadn't had to bother herself very much about him.

That Monday morning, Baker had remained in his room until just before one o'clock, when as usual he had gone out for his lunch. Mrs. Tickford had been in the hall when he came down the stairs, and they had exchanged a few remarks about the unpleasant change in the weather, and how bad it was for her sciatica. She had noticed that he was wearing an oilskin mackintosh and a black-and-white-checked cap. They were the things he usually wore when the weather was wet. He did not return home until a few minutes after nine that evening. At a quarter past nine he went out again — and then vanished into thin air, leaving his clothes behind.

What had actually occurred was corroborated by two eye witnesses. They were Mr. Jack Freeman, who lived in the house next door but one to Mrs. Tickford, and a Mr. Charles Hocknell, who lived next door to Mr. Freeman. The latter had been standing in his porch, trying to make up his mind whether to venture out to the Golden Crust for a beer or stay in front of his warm and cosy fire, when he saw William Baker leave his cottage. Still undecided, Mr. Freeman had watched Baker walk towards the sharp turn in the lane which led to the green. He was unable to see whether he reached it because it was very dark at this point.

At precisely the same time, Mr. Charles Hicknell, more enterprising than Mr. Freeman, had already been to the Golden Crust, enjoyed a couple of pints, and was walking up the lane towards the bend from the direction of the green, on his way home. Just before he reached the bend in the lane, he heard a cackling chuckle, a disembodied mocking laugh. He paused and listened but heard nothing more. He couldn't tell where the laugh had come from, but it made him feel uneasy. As he turned the sharp corner, he stumbled over something that lay on the damp and narrow pavement. To his surprise, he discovered it was a heap of clothing!

Back to Jack Freeman, whose desire for a beer had won over the desire for warmth and security. He had set off for the Golden Crust after all, but then had bumped into his neighbour standing over the pile of clothing, which consisted of a shirt, tie, socks, shoes, a set of under-clothes, a tweed suit, an oilskin mackintosh, and a black-and-white-checked cap. Mr. Freeman immediately recognised the cap and mackintosh as the property of William Baker. He had been wearing them when Freeman had seen him leave Mrs. Tickford's home a few minutes before.

Startled and not a little alarmed, the two neighbours had called Mrs. Tickford into immediate consultation. Complaining loudly at being dragged out into the damp night air, her curiosity compelled her to see for herself what the fuss was all about. She also identified the clothing as belonging to William Baker. But of the man himself, there was not a trace. In the very short time that had elapsed between the time Mr. Freeman had seen him leave his house, and the time Mr. Hocknell had stumbled over his clothes, he had vanished!

'The whole thing is absurd,' growled Simon Gale angrily as Zoe Anderson drove us back to Hunter's Meadow.

'Probably a simple explanation,' I suggested.

'But I don't like it. I don't like it one bit.'

'Maybe a practical joke,' I offered, to make conversation. 'He remembered your bit about the Snark, and — '

'Did Baker strike you as having that sort of sense of humour?' Gale snapped. 'Did he strike you as having any sense of humour at all?' He slumped into a corner of the back seat and thrust his fingers irritably through his hair. 'Something's not right.'

'Mr. Weston certainly took it seriously,' broke in Zoe, concentrating on the misty road ahead. 'When he came into the bar, he looked really shaken up. It's rather frightening.'

We had reached the top of the high street, and I directed Zoe round by the church and into the steep and narrow lane that led up to Hunter's Meadow. The headlights turned black hedgerows a vivid and startling green as the tyres hissed over wet leaves.

Rather frightening. I was willing to agree. But Simon Gale was easily riled, and I couldn't help thinking this was someone's elaborate joke to pull his leg. Was it Lance Weston's little joke? He was a good actor if it was. His shocked appearance at the bar had looked real enough.

And that heap of clothing. I suddenly recollected from the Hunting of the Snark: *In the midst of the word he was trying to say, in the midst of his laughter and glee, he had softly and suddenly vanished away — for the Snark was a Boojum, you see.*

Jack Freeman had heard a laugh, hadn't he? He'd certainly *thought* he had heard one. He'd described a cackling chuckle; a disembodied mocking laugh. All part of an elaborate joke? I wasn't so sure.

The open gates to the drive loomed up ahead, and a few seconds later we stopped in front of the massive iron-bound oak door of Hunter's Meadow.

Gale apparently was so absorbed in his thoughts that I had to nudge him before he realised that we'd arrived.

Only Trenton, the butler, was up. He took Zoe's coat, revealing her very attractive figure in a cream silk blouse and tweed skirt that accentuated her narrow waist. There was a fire in the drawing room, where sandwiches and a tray of drinks had been left for us. We took Zoe in there while Trenton fetched her suitcase from the car, promising to inform Ursula of her arrival. She warmed her hands at the fire, which Trenton had stirred into a blaze.

'I suppose I ought to have sent a wire or telephoned or something,' she said.

'Aren't they expecting you?' I asked in surprise.

She shook her head, and her face crinkled up into that little puckish grin that was so attractive. 'I thought I'd give Ursula a surprise,' she said. 'A spur-of-the-moment decision.' She stopped abruptly, her green eyes staring.

Simon Gale, completely oblivious to our presence, was striding about the big room, to the imminent danger of any small articles of furniture that happened to be in his way. His fingers were twisted in his beard, and the expression on his face would have made a gargoyle look angelic. It didn't surprise me that Zoe looked alarmed.

'Don't take any notice,' I said in a low voice. 'He's only thinking. He's not dangerous.'

'Dangerous, hey?' The word seemed to penetrate through to Gale's brain with a kind of splendid isolation, for he stopped prowling about the room and glared at me. 'It could be, young feller. It could be exceedingly dangerous.'

'Do you really think something serious has happened to that man?' asked Zoe, her hands plucking nervously at her skirt.

'I hope not, but I'm worried,' answered Gale. 'I hope Baker turns up tomorrow and we all laugh till our sides ache. But suppose he doesn't? I've a feeling this might be more than a joke.' He slumped into an armchair by the fire and scowled.

I didn't want to upset him so I said

nothing, but I thought that his preoccupation with the incident was arrant nonsense.

My thoughts were interrupted as Ursula Bellman came in. She was wearing a cherry-coloured housecoat of corded velvet over her nightdress, and on her small bare feet were slippers of the same shade. Except for the nightdress, she might never have been in bed at all. There was not a hair out of place.

She welcomed Zoe with delighted surprise. 'My dear, how lovely to see you!' she greeted, kissing her affectionately. 'But why didn't you let me know you were coming?

'I didn't make up my mind until the last moment,' answered Zoe, laughing. 'I just threw some things into a case and climbed into my car, and here I am! I should've let you know. But it doesn't matter, does it? I'm not putting you to any trouble, am I?'

Ursula waved such a suggestion aside with a graceful gesture. 'Of course you're not,' she answered. 'The place is empty except for Simon and Mr. Trueman

— and there would always be room for you.'

Zoe tilted her dark head to one side and eyed her critically. 'You haven't changed a bit. Not one bit, Ursula.'

Ursula gave an altogether charming and delightful laugh. Her beautifully pencilled brows rose slightly. 'It's been rather a long time, hasn't it? I haven't seen you since I married Joshua. To think at one time we were inseparable. How time flies.'

It all sounded very nice and charming, but there was a false note somewhere. I got the impression that in spite of her smiles and sweetness, Ursula Bellman wasn't as pleased by Zoe's unexpected appearance as she made out. There was no tangible reason for this; just some vague undercurrent I detected beneath the surface charm. If Zoe were aware of it, she gave no sign. She was as friendly as could be.

Zoe started to tell her how she had met us, and what had happened to William Baker, but Ursula wasn't listening. 'You must be ravenously hungry and terribly tired. I've told Trenton to take a cold supper tray to my room while he lights a fire in yours. We can have a nice cosy chat over a glass of something.' With that, she carted Zoe off.

Gale was still hunched up in the armchair by the fire, and only grunted when I spoke to him. With Zoe's departure, the life seemed to have gone out of the room. I'd had a long, tiring day, what with the confounded merger and all the excitement over Baker's disappearance, so I went to bed.

I didn't sleep well. Usually I drop off as soon as my head feels the touch of the pillow, but that night I lay staring into the darkness of the room and listening to a clock somewhere distant striking the hours. Eventually I did fall asleep; my last conscious thought was of Zoe Anderson's crinkly smile and the dimples at the corners of her mouth.

★   ★   ★

When I came down to breakfast on the following morning, Gale was standing at the long table in the dining room, staring at a letter that had arrived by the morning post. He took no notice of me when I greeted him, but continued to stare at it, totally preoccupied, twisting his fingers thoughtfully in his beard.

The weather had changed during the night. The sun was slanting in through the wide windows. There was a faint smell of burning leaves in the air and from somewhere in the direction of the sweeping lawns below the terrace, a haze of greyish smoke was drifting slowly towards the house.

Gale looked up suddenly as if noticing my presence for the first time. 'Come over here, young feller,' he growled.

He held out the object of his attention. I saw it wasn't a letter he had been studying so assiduously, but a postcard that had been enclosed in an envelope. 'What do you make of that, hey?'

On the card, neatly printed with a ball-point pen, was a single sentence:

The Snark <u>was</u> a Boojum.

The word *was* had been heavily underlined.

4

I tossed the card down on the table. 'Are you concerned about this?' I asked. 'Surely somebody's sent you this to make sure you don't miss the joke?'

I picked up the envelope. It was an ordinary rectangular white one, of the type that can be bought at any small stationer's shop. It was addressed in the same neatly printed characters as those on the card: Simon Gale, Esq., Hunter's Meadow, Lower Bramsham.

'Look at the postmark,' Gale instructed, stabbing his finger at the postcard in my hand. 'This was posted in Marling, in time to catch the five o'clock post — at least four and a half hours *before* Baker vanished!' Gale poured himself a cup of coffee. He took two large gulps from it and said irritably: 'This whole thing's wrong somehow. Can you imagine a feller like that planning such an elaborate joke? And if this *is* a joke, as you seem to insist

49

it is, it could only have been carried out with his assistance.'

I remembered the little nondescript sandy-haired man who had sat at that table and kept fidgeting with his spoons and forks, and I had to admit that there was something in what Gale said, but I wasn't about to yield to his opinion without a fight. 'Maybe someone else put him up to it,' I suggested, going over and inspecting the dishes on the sideboard and deciding on kidneys and bacon. 'If it isn't a joke, what do you think it is?'

'A Boojum!' answered Gale, slamming a plate of kedgeree on the table and sitting down.

I stared at him in astonishment, as if he'd lost his reason. 'Are you seriously suggesting Baker was spirited away by a mythical creature that existed only in the mind of Lewis Carroll?'

'Not a mythical creature,' corrected Gale, taking a mouthful of kedgeree. 'But a Snark, nonetheless. A dangerous and warped mind. A monstrosity, young feller — I've met them before.'

Maybe it was because I hadn't slept

very well and felt irritable and argumentative that I couldn't see the way Gale was accounting for the events as having much merit. 'Why should anyone want to get rid of Baker?' I demanded.

'Well if someone wanted to get rid of Baker — obviously we don't yet know why — I supplied 'em with an opportunity, d'you see? I triggered it. I gave 'em a plan.'

'I *don't* see,' I replied, coming over with my laden plate and sitting down opposite him. 'I think you're creating a mystery where there isn't one. Why would anyone want to get rid of him? I'm sure that before the day's out we'll have a perfectly acceptable explanation.'

Gale grabbed a slice of toast and stabbed with his knife at a block of butter. 'Before we can answer the *why*, we have to answer another very important question. Who was Baker?'

I stared at him with a forkful of kidney and bacon halfway to my mouth. 'Who was Baker — ?' I repeated, putting my fork down. 'He was just William Baker. I'd suggest no more and no less.'

'That's just the sort of remark I might expect coming from a lawyer,' he said, leering at me horribly. 'The question needs answering before we can go any further. Look here, he occupied a bedsitting room in a small working-class house, and he was obviously an insignificant little feller with zero personality.' He leaned forward, lowering his voice. 'Yet he was invited here to dinner with all the nobs of Lower Bramsham.'

I agreed that struck me as curious.

'Well I'm glad we agree on something,' he grunted sarcastically. 'I like oddities to be explained, d'you see? I want to know a lot more about William Baker.'

'Why not ask Bellman?' I suggested.

'Ask me what?' inquired the dry voice of Joshua Bellman. He must have come in very quietly, for neither of us had heard him. He was fully dressed, and he stood blinking a little in the doorway as though the sunlight hurt his eyes.

'Baker's vanished,' retorted Gale.

Bellman's small brown eyes contracted slightly.

'Ah-ha, that surprised you, hey?'

Bellman pulled out a chair and sat down. 'When you reach my age, very few things can be said to surprise you,' he answered in a level voice. 'Tell me about it.'

With great gusto and a wealth of detail, Simon Gale told him. Bellman listened without comment, examined the postcard, and shrugged his shoulders. 'You seem to have started something,' he remarked calmly. 'Of course, this is the result of what you said on Friday. Rather a childish joke, in my opinion.'

I looked triumphantly at Gale. 'I agree,' I said.

'Surely there can't be any question of taking it seriously?' inquired Bellman, his thin lips twisting into a faint smile. 'I should imagine it was probably Lance Weston's idea. It's just the kind of thing that would amuse him.' There was the merest trace of contempt in his tone.

I remembered Lance Weston turning up at the pub. He hadn't looked like the perpetrator of a practical joke. He'd looked shaken. The incident had plainly shocked him. I looked at Gale, and I could see he didn't think Weston was involved in Bakers disappearance either.

'What sort of a feller was Baker?' Gale asked, scowling at both of us.

'I know nothing about him whatsoever,' answered Bellman surprisingly. We both stared at him.

'You invited him to dinner — ' Gale began.

Bellman interrupted him with a sharp, impatient gesture. 'I invited him because he did me a service,' he said curtly. 'Beyond that, I know nothing at all about him, and I have no particular desire to know anything.'

'What service did he provide?' demanded Gale curiously.

This time Bellman laughed outright. 'You really are the most persistent fellow, Simon. If you must know, it was a very simple one. I was out walking in the woods, trod on a rotten branch, and sprained my ankle. It hurt like hell. I couldn't walk and would have been stranded if Baker hadn't come along and helped me.'

As simple as that! We left Gale

glowering fiendishly at an inoffensive dish of marmalade and went up to Bellman's study for another session with the acquisition.

★　★　★

Having missed her at breakfast, I had been looking forward to seeing Zoe Anderson again at lunch. She'd gone out with Ursula somewhere, however, so there were only Bellman, Gale, Merridew and myself, marooned at one end of the long table. It proved to be one of the dullest meals I've ever had the misfortune to sit through. Simon Gale, still immersed in his own thoughts, scarcely spoke a word throughout, and Bellman ran him a close second. Jack Merridew never said very much, and, although I tried to make some sort of conversation, nobody seemed the least bit interested, so I gave it up and joined in the general gloom.

There was only one bright spot. Bellman was going out in the afternoon, so any further work on the acquisition was postponed until the following day, which cheered me up considerably. I found it very difficult to concentrate on dusty legal clauses just then.

Gale went off somewhere as soon as lunch was over. I had nearly run out of cigarettes, so I decided to walk down to the village and get some more. I needed fresh air after that depressing luncheon.

The first people I ran into in the high street whom I knew were Mr. and Mrs. Hope. Mrs. Hope was shoehorned into a tailored suit, and Mr. Hope wore a suit of plus-fours in a hideous shade of ginger. They spotted me before I could find a way of dodging them, so I resolved to make the best of it, praying Hope wouldn't start another of his share deal sagas.

'What's this I hear, eh?' he demanded after we had exchanged the usual greetings. 'Something happened to that feller Baker?'

'It's quite extraordinary, isn't it?' added Mrs. Hope, hungry for any scrap of information, her eyes protruding and looking more washed-out than ever. 'I can't understand it at all. Fancy a shy little man like Mr. Baker taking all his clothes off and leaving them in the street. What could've happened to him? Where did he go?'

It was a question, I discovered, that nearly the whole of Lower Bramsham was asking.

And just after five o'clock on that Tuesday afternoon, that question was dramatically answered.

Lower Bramsham, having a small population, didn't have a railway station of its own. The nearest was Farley Halt, a good two miles outside the village, and remotely situated in open country. It consisted of two dilapidated wooden platforms, and a small booking office and a waiting room, both of which were kept locked up. Trains only stopped there by request, most of the inhabitants of Lower Bramsham preferring to go on to Marling Junction. It was a little further but less trouble. As a consequence of this, Farley Halt had sunk into dilapidation and was practically unused, though not totally neglected.

Once a week, usually a Tuesday morning, a Mr. Liphook, a railway official who combined the duties of station master, porter, ticket-collector and everything else, would ceremoniously unlock the small waiting room, sweep it out, and lock it up again. An emergency dental visit had delayed him until late in the afternoon.

When he unlocked and entered the dim and dusty waiting room on this particular Tuesday afternoon, he received a shock. Lying on the floor under the window lay the dead and completely naked body of William Baker.

5

Simon Gale first heard the news of Mr. Liphook's discovery. He was in a small white-washed cottage that did duty for a police station in Lower Bramsham, talking to Sergeant Lockyer and Chief Detective Inspector Halliday, when the news came in.

Mrs. Tickford had reported the disappearance of her lodger to Sergeant Lockyer, who in turn had reported it to the police at Marling. As a consequence, Chief Detective Inspector Halliday had come over shortly after lunch to find out more about it and make a few inquiries. He had been preparing to return to Marling with the meagre information he had been able to gather when Simon Gale dropped in seeking fresh news.

They discovered they knew each other. Halliday was the brother-in-law of Detective Inspector Hatchard, who was connected with the police in Ferncross, the village where Gale lived. They had met earlier that year and were reminiscing when Mr. Liphook made his frantic call, putting an end to gossip and conjecture and spurring them into action.

I was just out of the high street, on my way back to Hunter's Meadow, when I heard the skidding of tyres and Gale's booming voice shouting at me excitedly. Looking round, I saw he was leaning out of the window of a police car that had drawn up behind me.

'Hey, Trueman!' he bellowed, waving. 'Come on, get in!'

'What's happened?' I demanded.

'Get in! You're holding things up!'

The car door opened, and I moved to the open door to ask some more questions when an arm reached out and grabbed me by the shoulder and dragged me inside. I found myself crammed on a seat between Gale and a thin-faced man with greying ginger hair and a moustache who was wearing the uniform of a police sergeant. The car accelerated and swung round to the right of the green. I opened my mouth to protest.

'Baker's dead,' interrupted Gale. 'His body's been found at a place called Farley Halt. That's where we're going.'

'Dead?' I couldn't quite believe it.

'Not such a joke now, eh?'

A broad-shouldered, round-faced man who was sitting in the front seat beside the driver said, 'We're not definitely sure yet that it's Baker's body, sir. There's been no identification.'

Gale snapped his fingers irritably. 'Splitting hairs, eh? Of course it's Baker's body. You're not suggesting there could be two?'

'I'm not suggesting anything,' the man broke in. 'But we can't take it as a fact until the body's been identified.'

'Well Trueman and I can soon settle that,' retorted Gale, 'eh, young feller?'

We sped along a bleak and open country road. Dusk had come and it was beginning to rain. Away to the far right on the crest of a low embankment ran the railway line, and beyond that, a fringe of shadowy trees that was fast merging with a charcoal sky.

I was trying in my mind to picture what had actually happened. 'Assuming the body to be Baker's,' I said, 'where was it found, when was it found, and who found it?'

Gale told me of Mr. Liphook's grim discovery in the disused waiting room late that afternoon. Not a joke at all.

Farley Halt, when we reached it, turned out to be even more dreary and desolate than I had imagined. The entrance was up a slight incline, bordered on either side by ragged hedges that led directly to the narrow wooden platform via a swing gate. In the centre of this platform was a low-roofed structure, little more than a shed, that backed onto a slope of rough grassland dotted with trees and bushes. It was obvious to me that this was the waiting room in which resided the remains of William Baker. Remains I was about to come face to face with.

Across a double set of railway lines was another platform, bare and without shelter of any sort, at the back of which ran a fence of open wood palings. All around was nothing but an expanse of open country dotted with patches of woodland. A man I assumed to be Mr. Liphook was standing near the building. He looked more than agitated. He seemed at his wits' end.

'Thank the lord you've come,' he said. 'I don't think I could've stood it much longer.'

We all stopped, frozen in time, as a train pulling a long line of goods wagons thundered through. When it had passed, we all came alive again and followed Mr. Liphook to the open door of the waiting room.

If the outside had been dreary and desolate, the inside was worse. The paint, which had once been green and brown, had lost its colour and was worn and flaking. The fireplace was empty. Above it was a torn and fly-specked poster in a cracked glass frame extolling the virtues of the Lake District. Beside it was a single gas bracket with a broken mantle that wavered in the draught, the light alternately flaring whitely or dimming to a ghostly blue. There was a great damp stain on the floor where rain had seeped in through the discoloured ceiling. The atmosphere was dank and smelt of mildew.

Under the grimy window facing the door ran a narrow bench, in front of which lay the nude and twisted body of William Baker. Beneath one thin and narrow shoulder-blade was a bluish-red wound near which a little blood had crusted.

Chief Detective Inspector Halliday stared down at the corpse, his face hardened to sternness, aware of the maliciousness of a murderer who would leave their victim in such an undignified state. 'Can you identify him, sir?' he asked, without looking round.

'It's Baker,' grunted Gale. 'No question about it.' His bushy brows were drawn down over his eyes and his fingers were tangling and untangling his beard. It was the expression of a man filled with a fierce and terrible anger.

'Murder, without a doubt,' commented Halliday, bending down and examining the entry wound closely. 'That's where the knife went in.'

'Poor devil,' muttered Gale. 'This is what I was afraid of.'

Outside it was raining more heavily. The rustle of it on the fallen leaves and bushes was like the whispering of many voices.

'Where's that doctor?' asked Halliday impatiently. 'I telephoned Marling before we left. Should be here by now.' He looked at his watch. His eyes shifted to where a green-faced Mr. Liphook hovered by the open door, looking as if he might be sick at any moment. 'Is this place always kept locked?' he asked.

I looked across at Mr. Liphook, expectant for his answer, and saw a scraggy, wizened man with many wrinkles on his leathery face, nearly white hair, a worn peaked cap, and a uniform too big for him. No smart railway official would have fitted in with the dilapidation of Farley Halt. Mr. Liphook was a perfect match.

'Yes, sir.' Mr. Liphook pulled himself together with start. ''Cept on Tuesdays, when I sweep the place out. Like this afternoon.'

'When you unlocked it this afternoon,' said Halliday, 'did it seem as if the lock had been tampered with?'

Mr. Liphook scratched his pointed and bristly chin, looking down at the lock in question. He shook his head. 'I didn't notice nothing different. I put me key in like always. It opened right enough.'

'You're quite sure the door was locked?'

Mr. Liphook was certain the door had been locked.

'The last time this door was opened to your knowledge, apart from this afternoon, was last Tuesday, eh?'

'That's right, sir.'

'How many keys are there?' asked Halliday.

Mr. Liphook dragged a bunch of keys from out of his trouser pocket and held them up. He selected one particular key. 'Only this one,' he said.

'Would it be possible for anyone to get hold of your keys?'

Mr. Liphook shook his head, stowing the keys back in his pocket. 'When they're not with me, they're on my bedside table.'

'I see,' murmured Halliday. 'What time did you get off duty yesterday night?'

'Four o'clock,' answered Mr. Liphook, involuntarily clutching his jaw. 'My tooth was killing me. I couldn't stand it, so I went home. They told me this morning it was an abscess.'

'When does the last train go through?'

'The six forty-five from Marling Junction. I normally leave ten minutes after that.'

'The station was completely deserted last night?'

'It would have been, unless . . . ' Mr. Liphook looked uncomfortable.

'Unless what, Mr. Liphook?' asked Halliday.

'Unless there were any passengers set down.'

'Sergeant Lockyer, check with Marling Junction if any passengers got off here last night, would you?'

'Yes, sir.' Lockyer made a note.

Halliday walked slowly up to the window. 'Is this kept fastened?'

Mr. Liphook looked agitated. 'It's supposed to be,' he answered. 'The catch is broke. I've reported it. I reported it months ago.'

'Ah,' said Halliday, looking down at the twisted position of the body on the floor and noticing a contusion on the ribcage. 'I reckon the body was pushed through that window. You haven't touched it, Mr. Liphook?'

'It ain't been opened for as long as I can remember,' Mr. Liphook declared, unaware he was revealing the limited nature of his cleaning capabilities. 'It's been painted over enough times. It's stuck up tight.'

'I'll arrange for it to be examined,' said Halliday, as there came from outside the sound of voices and the thudding of feet on the wooden platform. The police surgeon, a stout man in a soft hat and damp raincoat, appeared at the open doorway. Behind him, just visible, loomed two other men.

'This is a godforsaken hole,' the police surgeon complained, uttering a clucking sound of disapproval as he pushed past me, his eyes taking a quick cursory glance around the cheerless waiting room before coming to rest upon the cold and pathetic body of William Baker.

Halliday smiled good-naturedly. 'I didn't choose it, Doctor.' He beckoned to the two men who had accompanied the doctor, one of whom carried a large equipment case. 'Jepson, Rogers, let's get these photographs done.'

Flashbulbs flared blindingly as William Baker was brightly illuminated and photographed from different angles. I turned my face away. Then the stout police surgeon stepped forward and knelt beside the body, which was twisted over, partly on its side. 'Can you do something about the light, Halliday?' he asked irritably.

Chief Detective Inspector Halliday produced a big electric torch and directed a beam of light downwards, over the doctor's shoulder. The police surgeon made his examination, grunting to himself all the time and throwing snatches of information back over his shoulder.

'Stabbed through the back with a thin-bladed instrument. Bleeding mostly internal. Death pretty instantaneous.

Dead about twenty-four hours; difficult to say for certain. No chance that the wound is self-inflicted — couldn't be done. Some post-mortem contusion on his rib cage. Must've occurred immediately after death to show up like that.'

He got up, brushing ineffectually at the knees of his trousers. He looked from the angle of the body to the window and pointed to it. 'The contusion was probably caused by being pushed through that.'

'Meaning he was killed here,' said Halliday.

'Not much fun moving a dead weight very far,' growled Simon Gale, shifting forward a little. 'Any sign of a head injury?'

The doctor whirled round and fixed Gale with a stare. 'What's that? Head injury? Why the devil should there be a head injury?'

'Well, d'you see,' replied Gale coolly, 'there was no cut in his clothes. They must've been taken off before he was stabbed, eh?'

Halliday looked interested. His eyes

narrowed. 'I see what you mean, sir. Whoever killed him may have stunned him, then stripped him, and then . . . '

Gale nodded. 'Easy to find out, eh?'

The stout police surgeon glared at Gale for a moment, outraged that the man had poked his nose in, and that he would have to get down on his knees on the grimy floor. He shrugged his shoulders in a *have it your way* gesture and turned back to the body. After an examination of William Baker's head, he grunted grudgingly.

'You're right,' he acceded, 'there's a contusion at the base of the skull consistent with being hit with something heavy but soft, like a sandbag. The skin isn't broken.' He straightened up. 'Anything else?'

'Thank you, Doctor,' said Halliday.

The doctor looked at his watch as if he'd spent too long there already. 'I'll be off then.'

'Tell the driver to come back here after he's taken you home, will you?'

The police surgeon nodded. 'I'll let you have my report in the morning.'

When he had gone, Halliday looked

relieved. He turned to Sergeant Lockyer.

'Arrange for the body to be removed,' he told him, then looked at Mr. Liphook. 'Is there a telephone here?'

'In the ticket office,' said Mr. Liphook helpfully.

'Let's all go over there,' said Halliday, looking round at everyone. 'It's not pleasant in here. Except you, Jepson — I'd like a sketch plan of this place with the position of the body clearly marked. And Rogers,' he addressed the other man, 'see if you can find any fingerprints — particularly that window, inside and out. See if it's been opened recently. It looks to me as if the paint's cracked where someone's forced it.'

I think we were all relieved to escape to the ticket office, though it wasn't in a much better state than the waiting room. The atmosphere was damp and clammy. There was an old-fashioned telephone screwed to one wall, and Sergeant Lockyer busied himself arranging for the removal of William Baker's body. The rain was beating down heavily now, drumming on the roof, and splashing and gurgling from a broken gutter somewhere.

Mr. Liphook seemed to have recovered a little from his ordeal, as his face was a more normal colour, and he was smoking a cigarette. We all stood in a group, waiting for what would happen next. Halliday was leaning against a narrow dusty bench that ran the length of the wall under the ticket window, deep in thought.

'Before we all split up, I'd like to get the facts of this thing clear,' he said. 'I'd like to know more about this business of a Snark.' He looked at Gale and then at me.

We described the dinner party at Hunter's Meadow, and Simon Gale's joking reference to the analogy between the names of the people round the table and the characters in Lewis Carroll's 'The Hunting of the Snark'.

Chief Detective Inspector Halliday, his round face quite expressionless, listened. When we had finished he said, pinching his fleshy chin gently: 'I've never read this poem you're talking about. But, from what you've just described, the circumstances of Baker's disappearance exactly coincide?'

'Almost,' corrected Gale. 'The Baker in Carroll's verses wasn't found dead, d'you see? He only vanished.'

'Well Mr. Baker vanished — but then he turned up in a very unpleasant way. And you say it's all because this Snark turned out to be a Boojum.' He shook his head as if saying the nonsense verse out loud was against every rule in the police force. He bit his lower lip. 'Somebody listened to you, Mr. Gale, and saw an opportunity. This is a very nasty murder.'

I remembered Hocknell describing what he had heard that night in the darkness of Goose Lane: '*A cackling chuckle, a disembodied mocking laugh.*' I jumped involuntarily as a gust of wind and driving rain rattled the shutter over the ticket window violently. Some dusty handbills on a ledge stirred with a soft rustle and a couple fluttered to the floor.

Someone very nasty indeed. Someone with a perverted sense of humour who had murdered William Baker and dumped his naked body with as little concern. Someone who treated murder as a joke.

6

Talking drums and smoke signals were a form of rapid communication. A method equally as efficient was used by the inhabitants of Lower Bramsham, because before nine o'clock that Tuesday evening the whole village was seething with comment and speculation over the vanishing and subsequent murder of William Baker. Fear began to creep like an invisible mist through the village, lurking coldly at people's elbows and making them look quickly over their shoulders in case there might be something behind them.

The news had reached Hunter's Meadow by the time Gale and I got back for pre-dinner drinks in the drawing room. Zoe and Ursula, who had apparently spent most of the day shopping at Marling, had heard all about it from the keeper of the local garage where Zoe had stopped for petrol. Both were bubbling over with excitement. Ursula, who had displayed a complete lack of interest in Baker's disappearance up to now, had a completely different attitude and was burning with curiosity. Joshua Bellman treated the matter with an indifference she found difficult to understand.

'Surely you must be curious?' she asked him. 'This is the most exciting thing that's ever happened here.'

'Somebody gets murdered somewhere in the world every day,' he answered drily. 'Why should I get excited because it's happened in the village?'

Ursula spoke what they were thinking in a voice with a hint of a reprimand. 'That's a very cynical point of view, Joshua, and would not be shared by many.'

'This is different to any other murder, isn't it?' said Zoe. 'It's on your doorstep, and it's gruesome and tragic, but also weird — like the characters in the poem.'

'Weird like a Snark!' cried Gale.

'Yes!' exclaimed Zoe. 'Like a fairy-tale gone wrong. Like something's leapt out of the pages of a book and committed this terrible crime.'

'A crime of imagination,' I added.

'Or a crime of deception,' suggested Gale.

'For which you were responsible,' remarked Bellman, looking pointedly at Gale.

'No!' thundered Gale, thrusting out his chin belligerently. 'I won't have that! I saw the coincidence and made an innocent comment. I certainly wasn't to know someone was listening with a cracked brain.'

Ursula caught her breath. Into her violet-blue eyes came a sudden look of comprehension and a flicker of fear. 'Someone listening? Are you suggesting the murderer was here at dinner, sitting round this table? Simon, you can't mean that can you?'

I saw Zoe's impish face change as her eyes moved quickly from Ursula to Simon Gale. Her lips tightened until the dimples at the corner of her mouth almost disappeared.

'That's exactly what I do mean, d'you

see?' Gale exclaimed. 'It's obvious, isn't it?'

'Rubbish!' exclaimed Bellman without raising his voice, which gave him more authority. 'It's by no means exact, by no means certain, Simon. What you said on Friday wasn't acted on until Monday, and then we are by no means certain that the vanishing of Baker wasn't some sort of coincidence. It probably had nothing to do with what you said. And if it did, you know how quickly things get about round here. There was plenty of time for half the village to have heard about it by Monday. I think you're all letting your imaginations run away with you.'

Ursula's lovely face looked relieved. 'Of course you're right, darling. You *must* be right. There must be a stranger.'

Gale didn't agree. 'You can't dismiss the possibility there was a killer at dinner with us. It's wishful thinking. They'll all come under suspicion, d'you see.'

Ursula didn't want to go back to their former conversation. She wanted to believe her husband. 'How could anyone at dinner have had any reason for wanting to kill poor William Baker?'

'Does there have to be a reason?' I asked. 'Maybe we're dealing with a cracked brain, as Simon calls it.'

'If that were the case,' declared Ursula with conviction, 'it couldn't be one of us. It couldn't be anyone who was here on Friday. We're not mad, are we?' She laughed.

'Don't run away with that delusion, Ursula,' scolded Gale, wiping the smile from her face in an instant. 'It doesn't work like that. The kind of cracked brain that may have done this terrible thing doesn't wear a label. Outwardly they would appear quite normal, d'you see?'

I noticed Zoe give a little shiver. Her hands were twisting a handkerchief in her lap and they suddenly gripped it hard. 'This is really horrible,' she said. 'I never knew the poor man properly but I feel compassion for him, walking out of his house and vanishing, only to turn up — only to be found in such a lonely place.'

Gale flung out an impatient arm, looking at all of us as if we were completely stupid. 'Of course it wasn't Baker who left the house at a quarter past nine on Monday night, walked down Goose Lane and vanished without his clothes.'

I must admit he had our undivided attention. We all hung on his next words.

He thrust forward a bristling and belligerent beard: 'Just as it wasn't Baker who returned home just after nine. That's as obvious as a wart on the tip of your nose, hey? It was the murderer!' he thundered.

Zoe gasped in horror at this revelation.

'It was the murderer setting the stage. Baker must've been killed last night at Farley Halt, and his clothes stripped off 'im, so that his killer, wearing Baker's mackintosh an' check cap, could go back to Mrs. Tickford's an' perform his trick.'

'How?' asked Ursula, frowning.

'Aha! That was the simplest thing in the world,' cried Gale. 'He was carrying Baker's clothes under the mackintosh, d'you see? All he had to do was to drop 'em on the pavement, strip off his mackintosh and cap, and slip over the wattle fence. Hey presto! Baker has vanished, leaving all his clothes behind!'

While everyone digested this, Gale whipped out his battered tin of tobacco and deftly rolled a cigarette, which he lit, drawing in the smoke deeply.

'It was a considerable risk to take,' commented Bellman. 'Supposing he'd run into someone. What's that woman's name?'

'Mrs. Tickford,' I answered.

'Mrs. Tickford, or that man Hocknell, if he'd been a few seconds earlier turning the corner,' continued Bellman.

'But neither of those things happened,' retorted Gale. 'I admit he took a risk, but it wasn't such a big one.'

'I can't understand why anyone would go to all that trouble,' I objected. 'Once Baker was dead, why the trimmings? Why take the risk?'

Gale leaned forward in my direction and pointed a finger at me. 'You've biffed the nail right on the cranium, young feller. Why? That's puzzling me.' He tugged his beard, and both his shaggy brows drew down over his eyes until they almost disappeared. 'Maybe that's where the cracked brain comes in. Maybe if we knew more about Baker, we'd have a motive. Maybe.'

'Excuse m-me, Mr. Bellman,' Jack Merridew's voice, with its slight stammer, broke in apologetically. He had come silently into the drawing room and was standing just inside the door. 'There's a long d-distance call for you, sir — f-from Glasgow. The one you were expecting.'

Bellman swallowed his drink and got up. He had, I knew, a large store and warehouse in Glasgow from which all his Scottish business was controlled. 'Excuse me,' he muttered, and hurried out with Merridew at his heels.

Ursula made a little fretful movement of impatience. 'I suppose that's the last we'll see of Joshua this evening. Why he can't conduct his business at normal times, I'll never know. I'll just tell Trenton to send his dinner up on a tray.'

Dinner was a subdued affair after the heated debate that led up to it. Instead of coffee after dinner, Simon leapt up and proposed an alternative. 'Let's all go down to the Golden Crust! I need beer, and lots of it,' he boomed.

I could tell he was overflowing with suppressed energy. I noticed Zoe brighten at the suggestion, but knew she wouldn't go if Ursula didn't. I could see Ursula's hesitation. I'm quite sure she wanted to go but wasn't going to appear eager. In a subtle but charming way, she conveyed the fact that the Golden Crust wasn't for her.

As for myself, I thought it was a welcome idea. I didn't relish spending the evening in the house. And anyway, Gale wouldn't listen to any excuses, seeking to override any in that overpowering way he had. Eventually Ursula gave up resisting and agreed to come with us.

While she and Zoe went off to fetch coats and wraps, I went round to the garage to fetch the car. It was still pouring with rain, but at Hunter's Meadow you could reach the garage by a covered way that old Bellman had specially built when he'd bought the house.

There were two cars apart from Zoe's: Bellman's huge Rolls and Ursula's

Humber. There was also an assortment of bicycles. Between the bicycles and the cars stood an incongruous contraption that was Simon Gale's motorcycle. Perhaps if it had been an ordinary motorcycle it wouldn't have looked so out of place. But it wasn't in any respect ordinary. It was a special product of Gale's own devising that he had constructed himself. He had assembled it entirely to suit his own ideas of what a motorcycle ought to be, and the result was extraordinary. It was painted bright orange and sported all kinds of unusual gadgets attached in the most unexpected places. Simon Gale, mounted on this appalling contraption and dressed in his usual flamboyant style, was a sight never forgotten once seen!

I had previously agreed with Ursula that I would drive her Humber to take us down to the village. When I drove it round to the front door, the others were waiting for me.

The Golden Crust was unusually full that evening. Gifford was talking to the large and impressive figure of Cranston, whose face was bent forward in an attitude of grave attention. They hailed us as we came in. We threaded our way through the crowded bar and joined them. The usual greetings were exchanged, Ursula introducing Zoe.

'But of course you know more about it than any of us, Mr. Gale. You and Mr. Trueman were at Farley Halt with the police, weren't you?' asked Gifford.

Gale lowered his tankard, from which he had just swallowed a prodigious draught of beer. He looked at Gifford over the brim. 'So you're interested in murder, eh?' he said with a peculiar intonation.

Gifford frowned. He didn't look too pleased. His hand went up and fingered his neat grey moustache. 'We're all interested,' he said curtly. 'As we should be when a murder's been committed right on our own doorstep. I was sitting right next to the unfortunate victim at dinner that night.'

Cranston nodded slowly. 'The circumstances surrounding the death of poor Baker are distinctly unusual,' he said in a beautifully modulated High Court voice. 'Such a bizarre — '

'Dressed up, I agree,' interrupted Gale. 'Underneath all that theatricality, it's just cold-blooded murder.' He finished his beer and waved his empty tankard at Beatrice, who, glittering like a Christmas tree as usual, was busy at the other end of the bar.

Gale turned back to our little group. 'Did any of you *know* Baker?' he asked.

'Knew him by sight,' said Gifford, shaking his head. 'I'd never met him before we dined at Hunter's Meadow. He seemed a very nervous man.'

'I'd never met him before Friday night,' remarked Cranston weightily. 'Not the sort of man you'd remember meeting.'

I could see that Ursula was listening, but I don't think she really heard a word. She was somewhere else that had no connection to us or the Golden Crust.

Beatrice, finally free for a moment, took Gale's tankard as he ordered a fresh round of drinks. 'You're lovelier than ever, Beatrice,' he cried with a wink.

Zoe caught my eye, and her face

crinkled up into that delightful puckish smile that I found so alluring. I glanced again at Ursula, but I could see she still wasn't with us. The door opened and I noticed her eyes flick over to it hopefully. Was she waiting for someone?

A few minutes later I had my answer. Beatrice had finished our drinks order. Gale was paying with a handful of loose change, which he had scattered on the bar while managing at the same time to hand the drinks out. Then Lance Weston came in.

He paused just inside the entrance to take off his hat and shake the rain from it. The light from the bar fell onto his dark hair. I caught sight Ursula's face. For a fraction of a second, before she had once more regained her self-control, a flame had kindled in her eyes. But she was back to normal in a moment. It was like life had been breathed into a waxwork.

Weston saw us and came over. He glanced at Ursula, their eyes met, and there was that flame again. It was gone in an instant, and they both acted casual and normal. But I had seen it and so had Zoe.

Joshua Bellman's wife and Lance Weston were in love with each other.

7

I sat before the electric fire in my bedroom at Hunter's Meadow, comfortable in pyjamas and dressing gown. It was nearly one o'clock. The rest of the household had been in bed for more than an hour. I had never felt less like sleep in my life.

The old house was very quiet. I had heard Gale, whose room was next to mine, tramping about for some time; and once something fell over with a dull thump. But there was no sound in the house now.

Outside, the wind had risen. It came sighing across the Downs, gathering strength before it buffeted the house, and hurled the rain with a noise like thrown gravel at the glass of the windows.

I lit another cigarette and shifted more comfortably in my chair, stretching out my feet to the warmth of the fire. In spite of these physical amenities, there stirred within me a vague and disquieting uneasiness caused by that momentary revealing look that had passed between Ursula Bellman and Lance Weston in the Golden Crust earlier that evening. Why was I letting it worry me? It was really none of my business if a young and beautiful woman like Ursula had married a dried-up old stick like Joshua Bellman. But I did worry. It had also worried Zoe. I had seen the flash of understanding come into her green eyes and the troubled frown that had wrinkled her forehead.

As I sat staring at the glowing red filaments of the electric fire, I wondered how long it had been going on and if Joshua had any inkling of it. I doubted he had. He wasn't the type to sit back and ignore such a thing. There would have been trouble. It was clear every time he looked at his wife that there was adoration and devotion in his eyes — and something more, I thought. A fierce and jealous possessiveness. Inside that withering body burned a flame that was as intense as the one I had seen leap up behind Ursula's eyes at the sight of Lance Weston, and it was all the more revealing because of the contrast between that moment and her usually cold and emotionless exterior. Ursula was playing on the brink of a volcano that might be sleeping but was by no means extinct.

I drifted back to the day five years ago when I had only just joined my firm as junior partner. Bellman had come into our office in Bedford Row and casually mentioned to my father that he was getting married the following day to a Miss Ursula Grant. After he had gone, there was a great deal of head-shaking and tut-tutting between my father and old Timothy Wyse. They had both disapproved of Joshua's choice. The main reason for this disapproval, so far as I had been able to judge from what I overheard, was the disparity between the ages of the bride elect and the groom.

'There's thirty-three years' difference between them,' I heard my father remark to old Wyse. 'That's a recipe for trouble.'

But there hadn't been any trouble. The marriage had turned out all right, with nothing we knew about to justify my father's pessimism. Until now — the revealing look that had passed between Ursula Bellman and Lance Weston I had noticed earlier. Maybe my father's prophesy was coming true after all.

I got into bed finally, and although I fell asleep pretty quickly, it was an uneasy and broken sleep that left me feeling tired and jaded when I woke in the morning, feeling less like tackling Bellman's acquisition than ever. So it was with great relief that I learned that the telephone call from Glasgow on the previous night necessitated a visit by him to his London office. He was fully dressed, had finished his breakfast, and didn't expect to be back until late in the evening. I couldn't have been more pleased.

He had just driven off in the big Rolls when Simon Gale put in an appearance, looking more flamboyant than usual. He was wearing an open-necked shirt of the most vivid tartan, with a bright yellow scarf knotted round his neck and a pair of wine-coloured corduroy trousers that were practically shapeless. When he heard that Bellman had gone up to London, he was delighted.

'Couldn't be better! You can come along with me.'

'Where?' I demanded.

'I'm meeting Halliday,' he explained. 'We're going to look at Baker's room. Before we can begin to hit on a motive, we've got to know a lot more about the victim. That's the first job, hey?'

'If there *is* a motive,' I retorted, helping myself to coffee and toast and marmalade. I didn't fancy anything else. 'If you're dealing with a nut.'

'That's the last resort.' He sat down to a huge plate of bacon and eggs. 'We'll fall back on that when we've exhausted every other angle. It's too easy, d'you see?' He took a gulp of hot coffee. 'There's a plan somewhere amongst the craziness. I can feel it. There's a method in the madness.'

He demolished his breakfast in a few mouthfuls, lit a cigarette, and sprang to his feet impatiently. 'Come on, young feller,' he cried. 'Finish up. It's time to go. I'll take you over on the back of my bike.'

I shall never forget that ride over to the police station. Like a lamb to the slaughter, I climbed onto the back of that infernal contraption. The motorcycle roared into life and shot forward. I almost lost my balance and fell back off it. It propelled itself along with a series of pops and loud backfires — explosions that threatened at any moment to blow the whole thing to smithereens and us along with it.

Clinging onto Gale for dear life, I coughed and gasped from the cloud of blue smoke that enveloped us like a smoke screen as we careered wildly through the countryside at breakneck speed. Gale had no regard for the safety of life and limb, and it was a miracle we arrived at the little police station intact, pulling up with a jerk that almost shot me off the pillion-seat again. I felt bruised and battered as I staggered off it, vowing never, no matter what the urgency, to ever get back on it again.

Both Chief Detective Inspector Halliday and Sergeant Lockyer came out to see what all the noise was about. Gale, quite imperturbable, introduced his beloved orange machine to them with pride, explaining loudly the merits and uniqueness of what could only be described as a death-trap that shouldn't be allowed anywhere near a public road.

I discovered our visit to Baker's lodging was purely for Gale's benefit. Halliday told us, as the police car took us to Goose Lane, that he had already been over there and discovered nothing additional to what was already known about the dead man. Except for a few clothes and personal belongings of no significance, Baker might never have existed.

Mrs. Tickford was cleaning the step when we drew up outside the house. She didn't look best pleased to see us. Complaining in her high, thin and unpleasant voice about the painfulness of her sciatica, she grudgingly led the way up the staircase.

I saw at once that William Baker's room was poorly furnished. The bed didn't look very comfortable. There was a narrow wardrobe and a chest of drawers of imitation oak, a round mahogany table in the window, and an armchair by a small fireplace. The floor was covered in linoleum of a hideous pattern, with a rug before the fireplace and a strip of carpet by the side of the bed. It was a room uncared for; a room no one would want to be in if they could avoid it. There were smears of grey powder all over the place, visible signs of Halliday's previous visit. Otherwise everything was as William Baker had left it.

'I'd be glad if you can take 'is clothes away,' Mrs. Tickford requested from the doorway.

'We'll arrange that,' promised Halliday.

'It won't be easy to re-let the room of a murder victim,' grumbled Mrs. Tickford without compassion.

'What did you know about Baker?' Gale asked her. 'Any friends call?'

Mrs. Tickford shook her untidy head. 'I never seen anyone. Kept 'isself to 'isself — nice and quiet. Always ready with a word if 'e 'appened to meet yer. Polite, like.'

'How long was he here?' asked Gale.

'Well, only three weeks.'

'Did he get letters?' Gale inquired, striding about the room and peering at things with a ferocious frown.

'I never seen any,' answered Mrs. Tickford, shaking her head and looking as if she had answered enough questions. ''E was always up early so 'e might 'ave got 'em then.'

'Do you have a telephone?' Gale asked.

Mrs. Tickford looked horrified. 'No, I don't! I can't afford one o' of them.'

Gale was peering malignantly at a few cheap paperback novels on the iron mantelshelf. He flicked through a couple as if he expected to find some sort of clue. I imagined a coded message falling out, and smiled.

'The post office may help,' remarked Halliday. 'I'm calling in on our way back.'

'It's almost as if Baker had taken care not to leave a trace,' I commented.

Gale rounded on me. 'The murderer was up here for several minutes,' he announced.

A cry from Mrs. Tickford interrupted

him. 'What?' she exclaimed, clutching at her chest while taking a gasping breath. ''E was 'ere? 'E was in my 'ouse? Lord. Oh, lord.'

Halliday gave Gale a warning look, and going over to her tried to sooth her, edging her away from the doorway. 'Have you finished here, sir?' he said to Gale pointedly.

Gale had finished prowling about. He was scowling at a brass knob on the bed, obviously disappointed at not finding anything — though of course, I reasoned, not finding anything was indicative of William Baker's character.

Gale suddenly swung round on Halliday. 'Did you find a key?' he asked.

'A key?' Halliday looked puzzled.

'Where's Baker's front door key?' repeated Gale impatiently. 'And his railway ticket? There was no one at Farley Halt to collect it.'

Halliday shook his head. 'We haven't found anything.'

'No, because the murderer took them!'

'I see what you mean. I'll tell Mrs. Tickford to get her locks changed.'

Gale shrugged. 'I very much doubt the Snark will be coming back,' he growled. 'To the post office, then. This thing's got a hold of me and it won't let me go.'

Back in the police car, Halliday turned to him. 'I don't mind admitting I'd be very glad of your help, sir. That business at Ferncross last year . . . '

'Inspector Hatchard,' remembered Gale.

'He was impressed with the work you did on that,' continued Halliday. 'Told me what a good job you did.'

Gale was hugely delighted. 'That was a pretty little problem, hey? Everyone had a headache over that.' He became suddenly serious. 'You know, Halliday, this is ugly, this business of Baker. I've a feeling we're up against something very bad.' He frowned and ruffled his hair. 'This joker who sends cards and makes nonsense verses come true. It worries me. It worries me a great deal.' His face looked grim. 'I think this is just the beginning.'

8

The post office in Lower Bramsham was situated halfway up the high street and combined a sweet-shop, newsagent and tobacconist. Miss Wittlesham, who looked after these varied interests, was an elderly and voluble lady with a highly developed sense of curiosity. Her short and frizzy hair was greyish-white and grew high on her forehead. She had a small button of a nose that seemed inadequate for the size of her face. Her conversation was punctuated by a series of disconcerting sniffs, so that she appeared to suffer from a permanent cold in the head. Her eyes, which had a steely glint in them indicating shrewdness, were constantly watering.

'Letters?' she repeated in answer to Halliday's question. She passed the tip of her tongue rapidly over her thin lips. 'Mr. Baker had quite a lot of letters. Yes, quite a lot. Mrs. Tickford wouldn't know about them because they never went to the house. Mr. Baker made arrangements to call for 'em here. Unusual, I thought at the time. Mysterious, I thought. But none of my business.'

Her declaration of *none of my business* was most likely an understatement. I thought Miss Wittlesham would make everything her business.

'Can you remember any of the postmarks?' asked Halliday.

'Oh yes, easily. They nearly all came from the same place.'

I noticed Gale's expression of intense excitement. He was having trouble repressing himself.

'The same place?' repeated Halliday to make sure.

'Yes.' Miss Wittlesham looked at him sharply as if he hadn't been paying sufficient attention. 'London WC2 — that's Covent Garden. That's where they were posted from. They were mostly typewritten — business letters.'

'Why did you think Mr. Baker's arrangement mysterious?' asked Halliday. Gale nodded with satisfaction. The question had been on his mind also.

Miss Wittlesham sniffed, and knowing she had the floor, took her time considering how to reply. 'Partly,' she answered, leaning forward with her knuckles pressed hard on the edge of the counter so that they showed white against her red hands, 'it was his manner. It struck me as furtive.' She stood up, letting this sink in. 'Furtive is what it was. You see, he'd never ask for his letters if there was anyone else in the shop. I notice things like that.' She leaned forward conspiratorially. 'For example, what was he doing snooping round the village? What did he do during all the time he spent walking about?'

'Well, what *did* he do?' demanded Gale, unable to contain himself.

Miss Wittlesham recoiled, giving him a suspicious stare. 'That's for you to find out,' she said with finality.

I consider that if I'd been stuck in that horrid little room, I'd have spent most of my time walking about — anything to get out of it.

The door of the shop opened with a

sudden jangling of the bell above it, and Lance Weston came in. 'Hello,' he greeted. 'What are you all doing here?'

'Avoiding the question,' Gale introduced Halliday.

'Ah yes,' said the detective chief inspector, 'Mr. Weston. I was about to contact you.'

'What about?' asked Weston.

'Just a word or two about this business. Nothing to be alarmed about.'

'Have as many words as you like,' retorted Weston. 'I know nothing about it.'

'Probably not, sir, but we have to interview everyone who was at dinner at Mr. Bellman's last Friday night. Just routine, you understand.'

Weston looked at Gale with that supercilious curl to his upper lip that was almost a sneer. 'Looking for a Snark, eh?'

Gale thrust his face forward aggressively. 'Seek and ye shall find!' he boomed.

Halliday cleared his throat and looked at his watch. 'I have to see the coroner about the inquest,' he told them. If you'll be in this afternoon Mr. Weston?'

'I shall be in all day,' answered Weston. 'I'm working on my book.'

'Then I'll come round at four o'clock if it's convenient. That's your cottage by the entrance to Goose Lane, isn't it, sir?'

Weston nodded.

Halliday looked round at Miss Wittlesham. 'If any more letters arrive for Mr. Baker, I'd like you to notify Sergeant Lockyer immediately.'

Miss Wittlesham promised she would. Lance Weston bought some stamps and a tin of tobacco, and with that we all trooped out of the shop, to her obvious disappointment.

Halliday left us standing outside the post office while he went off to keep his appointment with the coroner. 'Let's get some beer,' boomed Gale, looking in the direction of the Golden Crust as the police car moved off.

Lance Weston gave Gale a warning look. 'I wouldn't go there right now,' he advised. 'The place is full of reporters. They've descended on Lower Bramsham like vultures, and I'm sure you'd be the number-one target.'

'Damned reporters.' Gale looked dismayed, his notion of a tankard of beer dashed.

'Come back to my place,' Weston invited. 'I've got some beer in the cellar.'

Gale's face broke into huge grin and he slapped Weston on the back, nearly knocking him down. 'By Jove, that's an elegant solution. Lead the way!'

The three of us set off, tramping across the green towards Weston's cottage. I knew it wasn't just the promise of beer that had cheered up Gale; it was the opportunity to visit Weston's home and examine the man more closely in his own surroundings.

The cottage was quite small, with a narrow strip of garden enclosed by a box hedge, and a path of crazy-paving that led up to the front door. At some stage in its history the two rooms on the ground floor and been knocked into one, creating both a living room and a study. It was comfortably furnished with plenty of easy chairs, a large settee, and several nice antique pieces. There was a large flat-topped writing-table by the window, overlooking the back garden, and the whole place was full of books.

'Park yourselves down where you like,' said Weston, throwing his coat over the back of a chair and switching on an electric fire that had been fitted in the old-fashioned grate. 'Shove your things anywhere. I'll just nip down to the cellar and fetch some beers. Trueman, you'll find some glasses in there, if you wouldn't mind.' He pointed to a corner cupboard.

I found three pint mugs and set them up on a table. Weston returned with a small case containing six bottles of beer and set them down. Gale eyed them suspiciously.

'I make it myself,' explained Weston, opening a bottle and gently pouring the lively contents into a glass which he then handed to Gale with a flourish.

Gale looked approvingly at the white ring of live yeast forming in a circle on the top, and took a swallow. He smacked his lips and gave Weston a look of admiration. 'That's the best beer I've had in a long while,' he cried, finishing the contents of the glass and impatiently handed it out for a refill. He looked at Weston as if he was some kind of magician. 'You made this?'

'I've been doing it for years — only small amounts, three dozen at a time.'

'You're wasted writing novels,' said Gale. 'You need to open a brewery! You are to be congratulated, Weston. This stuff is good. It's very good indeed.' He suddenly changed tack and became very serious. 'Now tell me something. Why were you in such a state when you came into the Golden Crust Monday evening? When you told us about Baker?'

Weston handed me a beer and poured himself one. He took his time. 'I'd just heard about it from Hocknell,' he answered. 'I admit the whole thing shook me up a bit.'

Gale frowned into his mug of beer. 'But why?' he asked, staring straight at Weston, which must have felt very disconcerting. I got the impression of a big cat about to pounce.

Weston shrugged.

'But why were you shaken up?' Gale

demanded. 'Everybody else thought it was a huge joke, d'you see? What made you take it so seriously?'

'It never occurred to me that it was a joke,' answered Weston.

'That's what interests me. The first idea that leapt into people's minds was that someone was playing a joke. Why did you think differently?'

'I don't really know,' he said, concentrating on pouring the beer so that it didn't froth over onto the floor. 'Perhaps I think differently to other people. People don't all think the same, you know.'

Gale looked surprised that he had already finished his second glass of beer. 'This is really good stuff,' he said appreciatively as he thrust out an arm and handed the empty glass to Weston with a blatantly suggestive glance at the remaining bottles in the case. Weston smiled, took the hint and opened another bottle. Gale watched him pour it with intense concentration.

'Do you know anything about William Baker?' he asked abruptly, grabbing his third beer out of Weston's hand and grasping the mug possessively.

'Nothing at all. I don't think I'd seen him before that evening at dinner.'

There was something about his tone of voice that made me think he was lying.

'Strange nobody seems to know anything about him,' Gale said. 'When a stranger comes to live in an English village, the inhabitants usually make it their business to find out all they can. The first reaction is suspicion and the second is curiosity. Now Baker, d'you see, was living here for three weeks, and nobody — *nobody at all* — knew anything.' He scowled at the froth on the top of his beer. 'Or they do, but they're not saying.'

'We haven't asked everybody — ' I began, but Gale cut me short.

'You can take it from me,' he declared, 'that if anyone had known anything, they'd have talked about it.'

'Perhaps there wasn't anything to find out,' said Weston, pulling a pipe from his jacket pocket and polishing the bowl with the palm of one hand.

'He didn't just materialise in Lower Bramsham, hey? He lived somewhere else before he turned up here. Where did he live and what did he do? He must've been here for a reason. If we could find that out, we might know a lot more about why he was murdered.'

Weston got up and went over to a tobacco jar on the littered writing table, then began to stuff tobacco into his pipe.

'Do you think so?' asked Weston. 'Do you think there's a real motive? A reason why he was killed in that way?'

'Don't you?' demanded Gale sharply.

'No I don't — no motive, no sane reason,' answered Weston, lighting his pipe. 'That's why I was upset Monday evening. You all thought it was a joke, but I didn't. I thought someone very dangerous was on the loose.'

'It's not the insane part that worries me,' retorted Gale seriously. 'It's the fact there may be a sane mind hiding behind the nonsense of those verses, acting mad, playing us for fools.'

I got a glimpse of a cool and calculating adversary seizing on that chance observation of Gale's over dinner. I saw again the long, shadowed dining room at Hunter's

Meadow, as I had seen it on that Friday night, with the dim faces grouped around the table, softly lit by the yellow flames of the candles.

Behind which of those faces lurked the mind of a murderer?

9

When we left Weston's cottage I felt quite light-headed. Weston's home-brew packed quite a powerful punch. I refused point blank to return to Hunter's Meadow on the pillion of Gale's motorbike. He was a little hurt at my resolute refusal I think, but there are some things you must draw the line at. Nothing would induce me to mount that diabolical contraption ever again. I was glad of the chance of a walk in the fresh autumn air.

Gale passed me before I had reached the church at the top of the high street, popping like a machine gun and surrounded by evil-smelling smoke. He gave me a malignant grimace and waved an arm as he vanished round a corner with a loud bang. I lit a cigarette and walked leisurely on, when rounding the same corner myself I almost bumped into Zoe Anderson.

'Hello,' she greeted. 'Was that Mr. Gale

who passed me just now?'

'It was,' I answered. 'I came here on that orange thing he calls a motorbike, but I had no intention of going back on it. If he ever offers you a lift, I suggest you find some excuse and refuse — if you value your life!'

She laughed, and I decided it was a very fortunate thing that I had decided to walk back.

'It did look rather fearsome,' she said. 'I'm looking for a chemist shop. Is there one?'

There was, a few yards back along the high street. I offered to show her. The grey clouds that had hung about all the morning were thinning a little, and an anaemic sun was struggling through the haze.

Zoe was wearing a belted green raincoat over a high polo-necked white jumper, and with her heavy glossy black hair framing her small face, looked very attractive. She wasn't lovely in the way Ursula was, but there was something about her that was infinitely more satisfying. At any rate, I thought so.

She bought a few items at the chemist — hand cream and emery boards, I think — and we started to walk back to Hunter's Meadow. It was lovely autumn day. The trees were beginning to show yellow and russet among the green, and the air was full of the smell of autumn — that rich mixture of wet earth and decaying vegetation which, in my opinion, is only equalled by the scent of a spring morning or newly mown grass.

Our main topic of conversation was the murder.

'There's something evil going on round here,' she said. 'Any murder is horrible, but this is a travesty.' She looked up at me sideways through her long lashes. 'To think it might be someone who was at that dinner. Do you think it's possible?'

'Unfortunately I do,' I answered cautiously. 'But I can't imagine who.'

'I should think it's more likely to be a stranger,' she declared, 'like Mr. Bellman said. He's nice, isn't he?'

I'll admit I was a little surprised to hear her say that. It was a description that I should never have thought of applying to old Bellman. She was looking up at me again in that infernally disturbing way, and she must have seen something of what was passing in my mind, for she added quickly: 'Don't you think so?'

'He's a very shrewd businessman,' I said.

'I mean underneath that façade. That's really only all it is — a shell. He's surrounded himself with that, like a kind of armour, so that nothing can get through and hurt him.'

I remembered the look that had passed between Ursula and Lance Weston in the bar of the Golden Crust. One day soon, perhaps, he would need his armour.

Again she seemed to read my thoughts. 'What sort of a man is Lance Weston?' she asked abruptly.

It was a difficult question to answer. I'd only met him two or three times, and personally, I didn't like him very much. He struck me as being selfish, rather conceited, and altogether unreliable. I could imagine he would be completely ruthless if anyone got in the way of what he wanted. I chuckled. 'He makes 'remarkably good beer,' I said, being deliberately trivial.

'You're not committing yourself, eh?' Zoe's impish face puckered up. Between her thin arched brows appeared two deep lines as they contracted. 'Ursula's a fool!' she commented under her breath and almost inaudibly.

The thick and sodden leaves were slippery under foot, and the tall trees lining the lane that led up to the drive gates of Hunter's Meadow dripped with a monotonous ticking like a myriad of clocks.

'I'm not going to pretend I don't know what you mean,' I said.

'You saw it too, didn't you? I knew you did. I'm awfully worried about it. I'm very fond of Ursula, but she's her own worst enemy. She can be so stupid — she's always done the silliest things.'

'You've known her a long time?'

'Ever since I was eighteen. Ursula was a model — you know, photographed for advertisements and things like that — while I was studying at stage school. I was going to be an actress but it never came off. We shared a flat together.' Some memory deepened the lines between her eyes. 'Then an aunt of mine, whom I'd scarcely ever heard of, died and left me a house and some money. The family business.'

'The family business?'

'Soap,' she answered.

'What? Anderson Soap?'

'Yes, that's right.'

My mouth fell open. Anderson Soaps were famous for their special oils and fragrances. I assumed Zoe Anderson's family must be extremely well off.

'I'd always wanted to travel and explore, so I went abroad,' she continued. 'I had a wonderful time. I only returned to England last week. I thought I'd hunt up Ursula and see how she was getting on. I'd sent her postcards, and I heard she was married and living here in Lower Bramsham, so I thought I'd pack a few things and surprise her. If she'd been away, I'd have just booked into hotel for a couple of days.'

'And you landed slap bang in the middle of murder, intrigue, and God knows what,' I said as she paused.

'Yes.'

She was silent for some time and then she said seriously: 'I don't know how far this has gone between Ursula and Lance. I mean — we've got to stop it, Mr. Trueman. Somehow we've got to stop it.'

'I don't see how,' I answered. 'Has she said anything to you about it?'

She shook her head. 'She wouldn't. She knows I wouldn't be sympathetic — not this time.'

I looked at her sharply. She was staring straight ahead up the narrow lane. I almost asked her what she meant by *not this time* but decided against it. If she wanted to tell me, she would.

But she didn't. After a long pause she said, still looking straight ahead: 'I suppose she married Mr. Bellman because he was rich.'

I told her I couldn't imagine any other reason.

'I could,' she said surprisingly.

We reached Hunter's Meadow just in time for lunch. Ursula met us in the hall and I thought she looked a little cross.

'Where *have* you been?' she said to Zoe. 'I've been looking for you every-where.'

'You can't have been looking for very long,' retorted Zoe, slipping out of her raincoat. 'You were still in bed when I left.'

'If I'd known you were going down to the village, I'd have come with you,' said Ursula after Zoe had explained where she'd been. 'I only stayed in bed because I was bored to death.'

Her lovely face was petulant and disconcerted. Only twice had I really seen her come to life: when she and Zoe had come back from Marling full of the murder, and that evening, for a passing second, in the bar of the Golden Crust.

★   ★   ★

The rest of that day passed slowly and was rather dull. Ursula had promised to have tea with Miss Beaver and insisted on taking Zoe with her, to my intense disappointment. Simon Gale, who had lapsed into one of his morose moods, went up to his room immediately after lunch and remained there for the whole of the afternoon. So I was left to myself.

I settled down in the drawing room and wrote a long letter to my father, reporting on progress with the merger and telling him all about the murder, and adding what I thought was going on between Ursula and Lance Weston. I knew that bit of scandal would interest him after his prophecy. It was getting on for three o'clock by the time I had finished the letter. There was still time to fill, so I hunted up a book and read until I fell asleep in front of the fire.

I was woken by Trenton bringing in the tea. I'm not used to sleeping in the afternoon and I felt a bit woolly, so when I'd had my tea I decided to post my letter. It was the right decision. The walk down to the post office did me good. I'd just slipped my letter into the post-box and was turning away, when a voice hailed me from across the street and I saw the fastidious Franklin Gifford waving to me from outside the small village bank. I crossed over to him.

'Do you have a moment?' he asked.

I didn't have anything to do until dinner, so I was happy to give him some of my time.

'Come up to my flat and have a drink,' he suggested. 'I live over the bank since my wife died.'

He opened a smart side door and led me up carpeted stairs. 'I used to manage a bank in Marling,' he told me as we climbed to the first floor. 'Owned a house there too, but now this suits me fine.' He opened another door with a highly polished brass knocker and letterbox onto a small hallway with rooms leading off, and ushered me into a sitting room that looked out over the green. The room was like Gifford himself — scrupulously clean and tidy. Everything was highly polished and set out to a rigid pattern, like a hotel. It gave me the uncomfortable impression that nobody lived there. Gifford was obviously one of those finicky people who liked everything in its place, and if a chair is moved cannot prevent himself from unobtrusively sliding it back over the dents in the carpet that marked the exact spot it had previously occupied.

He gave me a gin and tonic, showed me several photographs of his son who was in the R.A.F., and pointed out a large and extremely badly painted portrait of his late wife that hung over the mantelpiece. She had been quite pretty, but there was a worried, haunted expression about her eyes.

'Any news about this Baker business?' he asked.

I shook my head. Had he asked me up here to pump me for information?

'Strange business, sending that card to Simon Gale. Do you think it's a madman on the loose? Have the police checked asylums to see if anyone has recently escaped?'

I smiled at Gifford's amateur sleuthing and wondered when he had found out about the card. I doubted if Gale had told him.

'If it's an outsider, an escaped lunatic, how did he pick up on Gale's remark regarding 'The Hunting of the Snark'?' I asked.

'That's true. Rather points to one of us,

doesn't it — someone who was at the dinner?'

'Or someone they relayed the story to.'

'What does Gale think? Strange fellow, isn't he — blustering sort of chap. I'm told he's well in with the police.'

I wondered who had told him, and put it down to the village grapevine. They probably knew about the card as well. 'He knows Detective Chief Inspector Halliday,' I said. 'This isn't the first murder case he's been mixed up in. There was some affair at Ferncross last year.'

'Oh, was there? As a rule police won't have outsiders butting in.' He went over and touched the frame of a picture that hung on the opposite wall, moving it a fraction of an inch. I could see he was excited about something. 'I've got a few ideas of my own,' he confided.

I wasn't quite sure what he was getting at. 'Ideas?'

'This Snark business — William Baker. When I've got something definite, I'd like to discuss it with you.'

I wondered why he had asked me up. 'Is that why you suggested a drink?'

'No,' he said, shaking his head. 'It was something quite different actually. I rent this flat from the bank — they own the building. When I sold my house in Marling after my wife died, I put my capital into some investments. I'm gratified to say they've proved very successful, very successful indeed. I wondered if I could draft a will. Could your company arrange that?'

'Of course.'

'I don't want anyone round here to know about it,' he added hastily.

'Of course I won't mention it,' I promised. 'I'm here for a few more days working with Mr. Bellman. Would it be all right if I telephoned when I have a few hours free, and we could go over it?'

He looked relieved, as if a weight had been lifted off his mind. I presumed his son would be the beneficiary. But I shall never be certain, because I never again saw Franklin Gifford alive!

10

The following morning as I came down the stairs to breakfast, the telephone rang. It stood on a small table near the front door, and I saw Trenton cross the hall to answer it. After listening a moment he looked round, just as Jack Merridew appeared at the door of the dining room.

'Chief Detective Inspector Halliday wants to speak to Mr. Gale, sir,' Trenton explained, with his hand over the mouthpiece. 'He says it's urgent.'

'M-Mr. Gale's still in his room, I t-think,' said Merridew.

'I'll get him,' I called, and ran back up the stairs, sensing a development. As I reached the beginning of the corridor, Gale came out of his room, and his bushy eyebrows shot up when he caught sight of me running towards him.

'Hey, young feller,' he cried. 'What are you doing? Going into training?'

'It's Halliday — he's on the phone,' I

gasped, catching my breath. 'It's urgent!'

Gale's face changed. He bounded past me and went down the stairs in several swift leaps, so that by the time I got to the hall he was already at the telephone.

'Hello, Gale here,' he shouted in a voice that must have nearly cracked the diaphragm. 'That you, Halliday?'

The telephone chattered metallically.

Jack Merridew, still standing in the doorway of the dining room, was staring through his glasses. His lean, lantern-shaped jaw had dropped slightly so that his mouth was a little open, and it made him look rather like an astonished owl.

'I'll be along in ten minutes,' cried Gale as the telephone ceased its chatter. 'Don't talk any more on this infernal thing. People listening, d'you see?' He slammed down the receiver and turned. There was a diabolical scowl on his face, and his beard seemed to quiver with suppressed excitement.

'Come on, young feller,' he bellowed, grabbing me by the arm. 'We're going down to the village.'

'What's happened?' I demanded.

'I'll tell you as we go,' he snapped. 'Come along — I'm in a hurry.'

'Yes, but — look here, supposing Bellman wants me?' I protested as he dragged me over to the door.'

'He'll have to do without you!' he retorted. He swung round on Merridew. 'Tell Mr. Bellman that Mr. Trueman has gone out with me, d'you see? Tell him it's very urgent, and I'll explain all when we get back.'

Merridew nodded. His eyes behind the glasses were full of curiosity. Gale was struggling into his dilapidated mackintosh and urging me to hurry up. By the time I'd found my overcoat and pulled it on, he was out the front door and halfway round to the garage, and I had to run to catch him up.

'What's all the fuss about?' I asked him.

'The Snark was about last night.'

'You mean there's been another murder?'

'That's exactly what I do mean.' Gale slammed his fist into the palm of his other hand violently. 'And it's partly my fault!'

I looked at him sharply. 'Your fault?'

'I should've anticipated it. It was the logical sequence, young feller,' he growled. I should've warned him.'

We had reached the garage, and we both pulled hard on the big double doors. Gale made straight for his motorcycle, but I went resolutely over to Ursula's Humber. I got in behind the wheel. 'I won't go on that damned thing,' I yelled.

He gave me a malignant glare and for a moment I thought he was going to go on it without me, but then he relented. 'All right, damn it, all right!' he cried, clambering into the seat beside me and slamming the door as I eased the car forward. 'It would've been quicker.'

I shook my head. 'This is safer,' I insisted firmly.

As we swung round the corner from the garage into the drive, I was desperate to pick up our previous conversation. 'You should've warned who?'

'Gifford, of course,' he answered irritably. 'For heaven's sake, put your foot down!'

'Gifford!' I exclaimed.

He cocked an eyebrow at me. 'Some-body called after you left him yesterday evening,' he said.

A memory of that neat and tidy flat — *too* neat and too tidy — came into my mind. I had a sudden vision of somebody walking purposefully up the stairs and knocking on the door.

'What did you mean by a *logical sequence*?'

He looked up from rolling a cigarette. 'It's Lewis Carroll, young feller. Do you remember what happened to the Banker?'

I wracked my brain in order to correctly remember the lines of verse.

'Don't overtax yourself,' he growled. Thrusting his cigarette between his lips, he dragged from an inside pocket a thin book. 'I bought this from a little bookshop in Marling.' He held it up for me to see: *The Hunting of the Snark* by Lewis Carroll. He riffled through the pages quickly and read aloud: ''*And the Banker, inspired with a courage so new, it was matter for general remark, rushed madly ahead and was lost to their view in his zeal to discover the Snark.*' D'you see?

130

Gifford was a banker, hey? I should've known he was in danger.'

I suddenly saw all too clearly. Gifford's words came back to me: *'I've got a few ideas of my own.'* I should have told Gale about this, but there had been nothing of any value mentioned; and in Gifford's own words: *'When I've got something definite, I'd like to discuss it with you.'* There hadn't been anything definite. I'd put it down to amateur sleuthing. Now I saw that if I'd told Gale what Gifford had said, it might have been sufficient to trigger Gale into action last night. It was with regret I realised it might have saved Gifford's life.

'What happened to the banker?' I asked, unable to remember the lines, and feeling horribly guilty.

He gave me a strange look out of the corner of his eye. 'You'll see in a minute.'

There was quite a crowd gathered outside the bank when we arrived, including some reporters with cameras. I could see Miss Wittlesham at the door of the post office opposite, her sharp, steely eyes glinting with ghoulish curiosity. I pulled up and we climbed out quickly. On guard, near the entrance to Gifford's flat, stood a uniformed policeman who came forward as we got out of the car.

'Mr. Gale?' he inquired, looking from one to the other of us.

'That's me,' said Gale. 'Chief Detective Inspector Halliday upstairs?'

'Yes, sir. I've got orders to take you up.'

Under the watchful eyes of the sightseers, among whom I noticed Mrs. Hilary King looking very shocked, the constable led us over to the side door and we followed him up the narrow stairs to the door at the top — the same door, with its highly polished brass knocker and letterbox, through which Gifford and I had passed only the previous evening. It was partly open now, and I could hear a mutter of voices inside. A stout woman in an apron was leaning against the wall of the tiny hall, staring blankly with a scared expression at the door of the sitting room, from behind which the voices came. She turned to look at us as the constable ushered us in, and her eyes were frightened.

There were four people in that neat and tidy room where I had enjoyed a gin and tonic last night — four people and . . .

I didn't see what was sitting in the chair by the fireplace at first. Halliday and Lockyer were standing in front of it, talking to the two men who had been at Farley Halt, Jepson and Rogers. They had been busy. Photographic equipment was scattered about. Halliday looked up sharply as we came in, and his good-humoured face was grave and set.

'Good morning Mr. Gale,' he greeted, and nodded to me. 'This is a nasty business, sir — nastier than the other. Look.'

He stood aside, motioning to the others to do the same, and then I saw. The figure sitting rigidly upright in the small fireside chair bore no resemblance at all to the immaculate and fastidious Franklin Gifford. It was like some hideous dummy that had been balanced there. His face had been blackened with some kind of shiny pigment, and the figure was in full evening dress.

133

I heard Simon Gale's breath hiss sharply through his teeth. He shook his head in disbelief. 'This is diabolical!' He stepped forward and peered down at the thing in the chair, his face contorted with suppressed rage. 'How was he killed?'

'The same method as Baker, sir,' answered Halliday. 'Stabbed in the back with a thin-bladed knife. No sign of any weapon.'

'He's followed every detail, d'you see?' Gale straightened up. His eyes, almost invisible beneath his drawn-down brows, travelled quickly round the room and back again. 'The cleaning woman found him?'

I looked to the open door and could just see the woman in the apron hovering out in the hall.

'Yes,' answered Halliday. 'Mrs. Bounce let herself in as usual when she arrived this morning. She was hysterical when she rang the police.'

Gale nodded. 'I can imagine,' he said, looking at the grotesque corpse. 'How did he get in? The murderer, I mean.'

'I think Gifford let him in, unless he

had a key,' said Halliday. 'There was no sign of a forced entry.'

'The first is the most likely,' grunted Gale. 'Gifford let him in — which means he knew him, d'you see.'

'I may've been the last person apart from the murderer to see him alive,' I told Halliday.

'What's that?' He looked at me in astonishment.

'Yesterday, early evening. Gifford asked me up here for a drink.'

'What time was this?' asked Halliday, very interested.

'Just after five.'

'Was there a reason for this invitation?'

I explained to Halliday how Gifford had told me he wanted to draft a will and asked if I could help. I considered that if Gifford had any inkling as to who the Snark really was, he wouldn't have let his murderer in — unless he thought he had the situation under control? I thought of several reasons why he might have wanted to confront the Snark. Who was waiting when Franklin Gifford answered the door?

'We found this, sir,' went on Halliday, taking an envelope out of his pocket. 'It was stuck in one of the dead man's hands.'

He opened the envelope and extracted a plain white postcard identical to the one Gale had received. On it were several lines of neatly printed verse in a ballpoint pen:

He was black in the face, and they scarcely could trace

The least likeness to what he had been:

While so great was his fright that his waistcoat turned white — A wonderful thing to be seen!

'I thought,' said Halliday, 'that you might be able to explain it, Mr. Gale.'

Gale gave a bitter laugh. 'It's another stanza out of the 'Hunting of the Snark'. The murderer is fastidious. He likes to get the details right.' He threw down the card onto a table, dug his hand in his pocket and extracted two copies of the book he had produced in the car coming down. He handed one to Chief Detective Inspector Halliday.

Halliday opened it up and glanced at

the title page. 'Thank you, sir — very considerate of you.'

Gale was flicking through the pages rapidly. 'Here we are,' he said, stopping at a particular page. 'This is how it goes on, and you see what a lot of trouble the murderer went to. *'To the horror of all who were present that day, he uprose in full evening dress, and with senseless grimaces endeavoured to say what his tongue could no longer express.'*'

'We found a dressing gown and some clothes on the floor in the bedroom,' said Halliday. 'I'm fairly certain he wasn't wearing full evening dress when he answered the door.'

'Not when he was alive,' agreed Gale grimly. 'I'm sure his killer dressed him up according to his manual.' He waved the book of nonsense verse in the air.

Halliday sighed in a rather defeated way, I thought. He slipped the book into his pocket and stared at the body. 'The press will have a field day with all this crazy stuff.'

There was a heavy palpable stillness in the room. I could hear the rasping of

Gale's breath as he continued reading the next few verses to himself. A heavy lorry went through the village. As it went past, the whole room shook with the vibration. The figure of the dead man gave a momentarily life-like jerk, toppled slowly sideways, and fell clumsily across the hearth.

PART TWO

The Hunting

They sought it with thimbles, they
    sought it with care;
They pursued it with forks and
    hope;
They threatened its life with a
    railway-share;
They charmed it with smiles
    and soap.

'The Hunting of the Snark'
by Lewis Carroll

11

Chief Detective Inspector Halliday's office at Marling police station was small and cheerless on that cold and frosty Friday morning, and rather overcrowded. In the chair behind the shabby ink-stained desk, fiddling with a pencil, sat Major Wintringham-Smythe, the deputy chief constable for the county. Facing him, his good-humoured expression replaced by a worried frown, and uncomfortably balanced on a rickety chair borrowed from the charge room, sat Chief Detective Inspector Halliday with an open notebook on his broad knee. Leaning against a filing cabinet, the fingers of one hand twisting his beard, and puffing furiously at the remains of one of his rank cigarettes to the detriment of the already stuffy atmo-sphere, stood Simon Gale. I sat near the window, from which a persistent and icy draught froze the tip of my right ear, and stared at the shining toecaps of Sergeant Lockyer's large regulation boots, planted firmly where he stood, almost rigidly at attention, beside the door. An old-fashioned gas fire in the small and rusty fireplace emitted a continuous high-pitched whine, like the last rush of air from one of those childish toys known as a dying pig, and filled the room with melancholy sound.

We had attended this conference at the express wish of Halliday. Major Wintringham-Smythe had raised no objection to our presence, though he had intimated quite tactfully that he considered it a little unorthodox, and that all matters discussed were to be kept strictly confidential. He was a pleasant-faced, dapper man running slightly to fat, with a bald circle on the crown of his head and a surprisingly deep voice for a man of his small stature.

Halliday had just completed an admirably concise statement of the facts, covering the ground from Simon Gale's humorous analogy at the dinner table at

Hunter's Meadow to the gruesome discovery in Franklin Gifford's flat on the previous day. In the silence that followed, the infernal whine of the gas fire seemed to grow louder and more irritating until Halliday turned it off.

The deputy chief constable, still twiddling the pencil between his fingers, looked across the desk at Halliday. He said, clearing his throat: 'It's incredible. Absolutely incredible.'

'Yes, sir,' agreed Halliday stolidly.

'I can't make any sense out of it.'

'No, sir,' agreed Halliday.

'I'll tell you one thing — it's going to be a damned difficult task to catch this blighter.'

'Yes, sir,' agreed Halliday for the third time.

'It seems pretty obvious to me,' went on the deputy chief constable, making little digging motions into the blotting-pad with the point of his pencil, 'that we've got a lunatic to deal with.'

'Plenty of rhyme and not a lot of reason, eh?' interposed Simon Gale, dropping the end of his cigarette on the floor and crushing it with his foot. 'I wish we could be certain of that.' He paused. 'But we *can't* be certain, d'you see?'

Major Wintringham-Smythe turned his head sharply. 'Can you suggest any sane reason for these two murders?'

'No,' answered Gale. 'But that doesn't mean there isn't one, hey?'

I didn't think Gale was being helpful, particularly as I felt we were both privileged to be there at all. I was listening, but determined, unlike Gale, to keep my nose out of police business.

The deputy chief constable frowned. 'Let's agree that it's very unlikely,' he retorted, 'if you take into consideration all the circumstances.'

'That's just what I am doing,' interrupted Gale, scowling horribly. 'And there's one thing that doesn't fit in with your conveniently easy solution.'

'*Easy!*' exploded Major Wintringham-Smythe testily. 'My dear sir, there's nothing *easy* about any of this. Good heavens! Indiscriminate killing is the hardest kind to track down. If we're up against a homicidal maniac, we're going to have our work cut out — eh, Halliday?'

'I agree, sir,' said Halliday diplomatically, with a warning glance at Gale. 'I don't think Mr. Gale meant *easy* in that respect.'

I couldn't help thinking to myself that tact was not one of Simon Gale's strong points, and diplomacy was probably out of the question. He seemed to be looking for an argument.

'Of course I didn't,' cried Gale, waving the idea away with a sweep of his arm. 'Only a blither.'

Halliday coughed loudly and came in hastily: 'You think there is a motive behind these murders, don't you sir? I mean a real sensible motive.'

'I don't see it,' insisted the deputy chief constable, holding his ground. 'Why all this pantomime stuff — nonsense verses and such like? How does this fit in with anything sensible?'

'It's out of sequence,' answered Gale, glaring at him.

The deputy chief constable frowned. 'Out of sequence? What's out of sequence?'

Halliday also looked puzzled.

Gale found a match, struck it into flame on his thumbnail, and lit another cigarette. He blew out a cloud of poisonous smoke. 'Well, d'you see how the murderer went to a great deal of trouble to keep the analogy of the nonsense verse authentic? The vanishing of Baker, the way Gifford was found, and all the rest of the trimmings. Having gone to all this trouble to get the detail right, why did he reverse the order?'

'Reverse the order?' repeated the deputy chief constable, dropping the pencil he had been playing with and leaning back in the swivel desk-chair.

Gale nodded vigorously. 'He killed Baker first and then Gifford. If he'd just been following the verses in order, he'd have murdered them the other way round, d'you see?'

Into Halliday's eyes came a sudden flicker of understanding and interest. 'I see what you're getting at, sir,' he said thoughtfully. 'If there was a reason for changing the order, then there must have been a plan. If you're just on a killing spree for the fun of it, why do that?'

'Exactly!' exclaimed Gale, grinning at him approvingly. 'Hole in one!'

'I see your point, Gale,' conceded the major, pulling his waistcoat down over his spreading stomach. 'But I think it's slender. Someone who's insane could well be erratic. There's no logic in it.'

'No, no, no.' Simon Gale shook his head emphatically. 'To an insane man the whole thing 'ud have to be done right, d'you see? Having got the idea in his mad head — a sort of *idée fixe* — it 'ud have to be carried out correctly down to the last detail. That's how that kind of crazy brain works.'

'Can you suggest a logical reason these murders had to be committed the wrong way round?' asked Halliday.

Gale ruffled his fingers through his hair and frowned ferociously. 'We don't know enough yet, but my first thought would be necessity. It became necessary to kill Baker first beyond the murderer's control. I'm certain we'll find a logical reason as information becomes available. Who was Baker? What was Baker doing in Little Bramsham? Why was Baker killed?

What was the motive? And why did the murderer think his little plan would have been blown sky high if he'd killed Gifford first? There's some sort of connecting link.'

I could feel his frustration like a negative energy force.

'What sort of link?' asked the deputy chief constable.

'It might be anything. Not much good trying to conjecture until we have some facts concerning Baker.'

The deputy chief constable turned his eyes towards Halliday. 'What's being done about that?'

'We've started the usual enquiries, sir,' answered Halliday. 'If any more letters arrive for him, I shall be notified at once, and I'm having the laundry marks on the clothing we found in his lodgings traced. It won't be long before we get results.'

'In the meanwhile,' said the major, leaning forward and once more picking up his pencil, 'there are these people who were at the dinner party at Hunter's meadow.'

'They're being interviewed,' broke in

148

Halliday quickly, 'and any alibis checked.'

'They're our main suspects at the moment,' went on the Deputy Chief Constable, pressing the butt end of his pencil softly under his lower lip. 'Quite obviously the murderer based his whole plan of campaign on what Mr. Gale said that night at dinner. I think we can take that as certain, eh?'

'Yes, sir. I don't think there's much doubt about that,' agreed Halliday. 'Particularly as Mr. Gale received that postcard.'

'Ah, yes, the first postcard. That narrows suspects down to those who knew Mr. Gale was staying there, eh?'

'Precisely, sir,' agreed Halliday.

'Therefore,' continued Major Wintringham-Smythe, 'the most likely person to be the murderer is someone who was present on that occasion. That's common sense.' He looked from one to the other as if he expected some sign of approval. If he did, he was disappointed.

Simon Gale was staring into the now-silent gas fire. Halliday had dropped his eyes to his notebook and was scribbling down some sudden thought. Sergeant Lockyer, a picture of official stolidity, was staring straight in front of him, his thin face devoid of any expression whatever. I was wondering how this small group were ever going to solve this ghastly crime. Each behaving in their own way, they seemed incompetent to do so. Was my participation to be rewarded with an exercise in abject failure?

'Of course we can't rule out the possibility your Snark analogy leaked out, in which case we have to look further afield.' The deputy chief constable frowned at this idea. 'You'll have to get a move on. The newspapers are going to sensationalise this to the hilt. We've got to show we're getting somewhere, or the chief constable will insist on calling in the help of Scotland Yard.'

I saw Halliday's face turn to stone. Major Wintringham-Smythe nodded, pleased at the effect of his threat. 'You know what Sir Bertram is like, I see. He's only interested in results.'

'We'll get them, sir.'

The room fell silent as they pondered the prospect of failure and degradation. Suddenly Simon Gale's voice boomed out: "*They sought it with thimbles, they sought it with care; they pursued it with forks and hope; they threatened its life with a railway-share; they charmed it with smiles and soap.*"

I went cold. '*Smiles and soap*'? I thought of Zoe Anderson and her family business. Was it possible she was mixed up in this? It suddenly felt like I had walked out of the normal world through a looking-glass, to a place where everything was turned upside down, bizarre and illogical. But that of course was exactly the environment the Snark wanted to achieve.

Major Wintringham-Smythe completely misinterpreted what Gale was getting at. The major's shiny and well-shaven cheeks flushed with anger. 'Really, sir, I do not think this an appropriate occasion for levity.'

Gale looked at him in astonishment. 'I didn't mean it that way,' he cried. 'It's most appropriate, d'you see? That's Lewis

Carroll's formula for hunting a Snark.'

'I don't think it will be of much use in catching our particular brand of Snark, Mr. Gale,' remarked Halliday with a sharp look that intimated if he wanted to remain working with the police he'd better tone down his attitude in front of the deputy chief constable.

'You don't think so? If you want to catch a Snark, think like a Snark?' He leaned forward across the filing cabinet, thrusting out his bearded chin and pointing his words with a stabbing forefinger. 'Everything has a pattern, d'you see? There's one here if we can find it. D'you know what a palimpsest is?'

We all stared blankly at him.

'Well, I'll tell you. A palimpsest is an old parchment, or something similar, on which the original writing or design has been erased to make room for something else. If you take enough trouble and go about it the right way, you can decipher the original stuff beneath the superimposed material. That's what we've got here. We have to discover the original design beneath all the superimposed stuff.'

The telephone rang with a persistent and urgent shrillness. The deputy chief constable reached out his arm and plucked the receiver from its rest, listened to the voice at the other end, and handed the receiver to Halliday. 'It's Detective Constable Hammond for you.'

'Halliday here. Oh yes.' His face changed as the telephone chattered excitedly and he picked up a pencil to make some notes. 'All right, I've got that. Yes. Well that's very useful. We can work on that. Stay there and I'll get back as soon as I can.'

Halliday put the receiver slowly and carefully back on its rest. He looked at them with satisfaction. 'This morning a letter arrived at the post office for William Baker. The station was notified and the letter was collected by Hammond.'

Gale could contain himself no longer. 'For the love of Mike!' he burst out. 'Get to the point, man! What did it tell you about Baker?'

'It told us what Baker's business was.'

'Now we're getting somewhere,' cried

153

Gale. 'What was his business?'

'He was a private detective.'

To the astonishment of Major Wintringham-Smythe, Simon Gale greeted Halliday's announcement with a loud and delighted whoop of joy. 'What price your homicidal maniac now!' he cried. 'The beginning of a pattern is emerging. D'you see a glimpse of what lies beneath the surface? A neat fit, eh? A private eye snooping about Lower Bramsham, and somebody was afraid.' He smacked his fist into the palm of his other hand. 'Somebody was afraid of what he might find out.'

I could see that the police didn't approve of Gale's unrestrained zeal. Nevertheless he was right, in my opinion. At last, a positive break in this stymied investigation. Someone was afraid of William Baker, who was not at all what he seemed. I could share Gale's excitement. Vividly there came into my mind again a picture of that fleeting exchange of glances between Ursula Bellman and Jack Weston when their masks had slipped. Had William Baker been working for old

Joshua Bellman? Did he suspect? I paused, realising I was getting carried away. Murder was a bit of an extreme way to conceal an affair, and it didn't explain the death of Franklin Gifford.

'The same thing struck me the moment I knew Baker's profession,' said Halliday, nodding slowly. 'But it doesn't tell us much. It was only a note asking Baker to contact his office.'

'Who wrote it?' demanded the deputy chief constable.

'It doesn't matter two pen'worth of pickled walnuts who wrote it,' interrupted Gale impatiently. 'A private eye doesn't work for himself — somebody's got to hire him!' he glared at Halliday. 'What's the office address?'

'16a Gilder's Court, Fetter Lane,' Halliday answered, referring to his hastily scribbled notes. 'That's not all. A telegram arrived shortly after from a Mr. James Lawson. It was sent from Chancery Lane at 9.55 and read: HOPE YOU ARE ALRIGHT STOP TELEPHONE TO CONFIRM STOP JAMES.'

'We'd better contact the City of London

police,' said the deputy chief constable. 'Ask them to institute enquiries.'

I saw a gleam come into Gale's eye as an expression of malignant and unholy joy contorted his face. 'Rules, regulations, routine and red tape!' he exclaimed derisively. He cocked an eye at me. 'Come along, young feller,' he commanded, flinging the door open. 'You and I are going Snark-hunting.' With that, Gale was on his way.

I bid a hasty goodbye to Halliday and the deputy chief constable and followed him. As I closed the door, I heard Major Wintringham-Smythe round on Halliday. 'That fellow's stark raving mad! I don't ever want to see him again. For all we know, he's the Snark! It was all his idea in the first place, wasn't it?'

Gale was waiting for me impatiently on the pavement outside the police station, tugging his beard and scowling. 'Come on,' he grunted, grabbing me by the arm and striding off down the street at a pace I had trouble keeping up with.

'Where are we going in such a hurry?' I asked.

'To catch a train,' he cried.

I realised at once what was happening. We were going to London to visit Baker's offices in Gilder's Court and steal a march on Halliday.

'We're going to London right now?'

'Of course right now!' he answered. 'Why would we delay, eh?'

'That's all very well,' I protested rather breathlessly, 'but I have a job to do. I ought to be at Hunter's Meadow working on Bellman's merger.'

Gale waved Hunter's Meadow and Joshua Bellman out of existence with a dismissive gesture that almost knocked over an innocent passerby. 'I'll sort it out,' he growled. 'I'll explain to Bellman when we get back. This is urgent, d'you see? The blessed acquisition can wait.'

I didn't think Bellman would agree that his acquisition could wait, but arguing with Simon Gale, I had quickly discovered, was a definite waste of time and energy. Of course I felt relieved that Gale was going to put things right with Bellman — I didn't want to miss anything.

When we reached Marling Junction, we had a twenty-minute wait for the next train to London. Gale bought two first-class tickets, ignoring my efforts to pay for my own. 'Do you see a post-box anywhere?' he asked me, scanning the area.

'There's one outside the entrance. A short way along the wall, on the left.'

Then he propelled me into the station buffet, where he ordered beer. 'I'll be back in a minute,' he said, and went off in a hurry.

When he came back he looked pleased with himself. 'The last post goes at five forty-five. Whoever killed Baker intended to kill him — it was premeditated. I'll bet you all the gold in the Klondike that the postcard was posted in that box out there, before the departure of the last train. Now assuming he didn't magic the postcard out of thin air, he had it with him,' he said, then downed his pint at a single draught and immediately ordered another.

'William Baker was on the train?'

'Well would you lug a deadweight body

up all those steps and along to a waiting room? Yes, young feller, Baker was on the last train, and so was the Snark!'

'What about the ticket office?'

Gale growled. 'Not helpful. Just asked — no one there was on duty Monday night. Halliday can sort that out.' He picked up his beer and took a huge draught.

I looked at my watch. 'We've got two minutes.'

'Now, young feller,' Gale said, finishing his beer, 'this is where your firm comes in.'

'My firm?'

'We can't just walk into Baker's offices and start demanding answers to questions. We're not the police.'

I suddenly felt apprehensive. What was Gale up to now?

'No, we can't just walk in. We need validity.'

'You want us to pretend to be solicitors?' I asked.

He began walking towards the door of the buffet. 'Well, you don't need to pretend,' he growled. 'You *are* a solicitor.'

'Solicitors aren't police,' I said cautiously, following him. 'It all rather depends on who we're talking to.'

'We'll give it our best shot,' insisted Gale, dismissing any sort of caution.

The train came in as we reached the platform, announcing its presence by letting off steam with a continuous and eldritch shriek. Gale found an empty compartment and, ensconcing himself in a corner by the window, began to roll one of his poisonous cigarettes. I took the seat opposite to him and lit one of my own as a slight measure against the acrid clouds of smoke with which he was soon contaminating the air.

The ear-splitting din from the engine ceased abruptly. The train gave a sudden convulsive jerk forward and stopped again. The engine emitted a series of blasts and the train began to move, this time more smoothly, sliding out of the station with gathering speed.

Simon Gale was scowling out of the window with his bushy brows drawn low over his eyes and the fingers of one hand twining in and out of his beard.

Apparently he was entirely occupied with his thoughts. Settling back, I began to ponder the problem that had bothered me ever since I'd discovered what William Baker's profession had been. Should I tell Gale what I had seen that night in the saloon bar of the Golden Crust? Normally I wouldn't have dreamed of disclosing to anyone something of that nature I had inadvertently witnessed. But this was a murder investigation. I glimpsed in my mind the naked contorted body of William Baker in the dismal waiting room at Farley Halt and the grotesquely dressed-up corpse of Franklin Gifford in his flat above the bank, and decided to tell Gale what I had seen.

'Ursula Bellman and young Weston? Do you think I missed that one, hey? It was so instantly obvious that a one-eyed sailor with a patch over the other eye could've seen it!' he retorted ungraciously.

'I thought we were the only — '

'You and that woman, Zoe?' he interjected unkindly. 'You've been worrying, eh? You think old Bellman hired

Baker to keep an eye on his wife? It's quite possible you're right. You think Ursula and Weston had a pretty good motive for getting rid of Baker, hey?'

'That seems a bit extreme,' I ventured.

Gale leaned forward. 'I agree. It doesn't quite fit. What about Gifford, hey?'

'Exactly,' I responded. 'Too simple.' Then I thought I saw the answer. 'Too obvious,' I said excitedly. 'If Bellman had engaged Baker to spy on his wife, and just Baker had been killed, Bellman would have guessed straight away who was responsible. Maybe Gifford was murdered as a cover-up to throw everyone off the scent, concealing the real motive.'

Gale scowled at me. 'Rubbish!' he cried.

The train, heralded by a piercing and prolonged scream from its whistle, roared into a tunnel, and darkness descended upon the compartment. A musty smell like mildewed leather seeped in from the window and mingled with the smoke of Gale's acrid tobacco; then the lights came on.

'You won't get me to believe all this

Snark stuff was done solely for the purpose of hoodwinking Bellman,' Gale said. 'He's no fool. He'd have seen through it.'

'Perhaps he has. He's not likely to broadcast that knowledge, is he? He'd have kept it to himself.'

The train exited the tunnel and into a steep cutting. I leaned forward and opened the window as Gale rolled another cigarette. 'Ursula's bored to death in that place,' he said. 'She's just looking for excitement — but that doesn't make her a cold-blooded murderess. You've got to be depraved to commit murders like these. It takes a special type of person to treat human beings like that. And there's another snag. Neither of 'em could be certain that getting rid of Baker would have the desired effect. It might only postpone their little love-in-a-cottage from being discovered — all far too risky.' He lit his cigarette and flicked the used match out of the window, then drew in a deep inhalation of smoke and let it trickle slowly through his nostrils. 'For all they knew, Baker could have already made his report.'

'Who's this fellow James Lawson?' I asked, thinking aloud.

'Someone who's heard about the goings-on in Lower Bramsham and is worried for Baker's safety.'

12

Gilder's Court was a dingy little cul-de-sac about halfway up the left hand side of Fetter Lane. Apart from the fact that it was more grimy and lacking in paint, it differed little from the innumerable courts and alleys with which this part of the City of London abounds.

Next to a small shop selling office equipment, with a window filled with bargains in typing paper, envelopes, files, and all sorts of office equipment, was a wholly uninviting doorway. On the cracked glass transom had been painted 16a.

'This must be the place,' said Gale, scowling at the unprepossessing doorway with obvious distaste. 'Bit of a dump, hey?'

We entered a narrow and very short passage at the end of which was a smarter-looking door painted glossy black. On the upper portion of the door, of ground glass, was displayed in gold letters: 'St. Dunstan Investigations'. I noted that in contrast to the shabby nondescript exterior, this door looked quite smart and newly painted. I had no idea what to expect.

Gale turned the door handle and entered. We walked into a vestibule that led to inner offices and stairs to upper floors. The office furniture in reception looked new and of good quality. Everything was clean and tidy. The impression I got was of a medium-sized prosperous business. An attractive dark-haired woman, whom I estimated to be in her late twenties, was seated behind an enquiries desk, busy typing. She stopped as we came in, looked up at us, and did her best to smile. I visualised this woman typing the addresses on the letters sent to Baker at Lower Bramsham and posting them at a WC2 post-box. I produced my own business card, and in my best superior manner handed it to her.

'Trueman, Hartly, Ward and Trueman,' she read out, looking from one to the other of us.

'I'm Mr. Trueman,' I said, smiling with as much confidence as I could muster.

Noting I represented a well-established firm of London solicitors, she behaved in a respectful manner, but was slightly wary, as if she expected me to hand her a subpoena at any moment. 'How can I help you gentlemen?'

I cleared my throat, aware I was about to embark on a charade that could conceivably end my short career. 'We're here to see Mr. Baker,' I began.

Her face went ashen. I could almost feel her struggling to pull herself together. *She knows*, I thought.

'Mr. Baker?' she repeated hesitantly, staring at my card and frowning.

'Mr. William Baker,' I clarified in my best solicitor's voice.

'Are you certain you've come to the right address?' she asked me rather feebly.

'Quite certain,' I replied, sensing she was unsure of her ground and beginning to feel uneasy myself.

She took a deep breath, looked again at my card, and shook her head. 'Well, nobody called William Baker works here.'

I stood frozen as my heart sank. All I could immediately think of was that we had come all this way for nothing, due to Simon Gale's impetuousness. This had turned out to be a dead end.

'You probably don't know him as William Baker,' boomed Gale, butting in. 'I think he's working incognito at Lower Bramsham.'

'Lower Bramsham?' Now she looked positively alarmed. 'Where those murders have been committed?'

To say I felt we were treading on thin ice would have been an understatement. I could feel the ice cracking beneath us and expected to sink into freezing-cold water at any moment.

Gale didn't seem at all bothered. 'I think you've hit the nail on the head,' he cried. 'A very nasty business.'

'What has this to do with us?' quizzed the dark woman, tears gathering in her eyes. 'What exactly is it you want?'

'It's confidential,' answered Gale.

'Everything here is confidential, Mr. — er . . .'

'Simon Gale.'

'What can we do for you, Mr. Gale?'

'I want to see James Lawson in connection with the murder of William Baker in Lower Bramsham,' he replied bluntly, blowing sky-high any further pretence. 'It may not be a good time, but it's very important I see him.'

She looked shocked, pulled herself together, pushed her chair back, picked up my card, and stood up defensively. 'Please wait here. I'll be back in a moment.'

I had no idea how much they knew, but I was certain they knew something of what had happened. I gave Gale a look that implied 'wait and see'.

The woman climbed the stairs to the next floor. We heard her give a gentle knock on a door, a voice from inside, and the door open and close. Low voices escaped from within. We waited expectantly. When the receptionist returned she was subdued, but had that look of relief that comes when responsibility has been handed over to a higher authority.

'If you will follow me gentlemen, Mr. Lawson has agreed to see you now.'

I exchanged glances with Gale. We both realised we were about to meet the sender of the telegram to William Baker. From the way she spoke, I had the feeling that he was reluctant to see us, but in the circumstances couldn't refuse. This reluctance was quite understandable if they had already been informed of the fate that William Baker, presumably one of their own, had suffered. This entire office must be in mourning — in a state of shock. I couldn't help feel a small boost in my confidence that our journey had not been for nothing, and that we were in the right place, and on track. Who was this James Lawson we were about to meet?

We were shown into an elegant room with polished wooden filing cabinets along one wall. The man sitting behind a large mahogany desk was obviously shattered. His face looked white and drawn, haggard as only the recipient of devastating news can become in a very short while.

'Please take a seat, gentlemen,' he suggested grimly. He glanced at my business card, then at me. 'I respect your firm,' he said, 'and I have respect for your father, whom we've worked for on several occasions. If we'd met in different circumstances, things would be different. As it is, I've recently received a call from the City of London Police, who confirmed my worst fears. My nephew has been murdered in the most despicable way. You'll know him as William Baker, I think, but that's a name he works under — a pseudonym. His real name is Robert Lawson.'

I sat digesting this news, acutely aware both of us had blundered into a sensitive situation under false pretences, where if our presence were handled in Gale's usual tactless way we could be shown the door not only by St. Dunstan Investigations, but by Chief Detective Inspector Halliday, and possibly my own firm. Gale looked like the cat that got the cream.

'We're helping the police with their investigations.' I opened hastily. 'We have to try and unravel this mystery and catch this killer before anyone else dies. Do you have any idea what Baker, your nephew, was doing in Lower Bramsham?'

'I can only tell you Felicity received a telephone call — Felicity from reception; the woman who showed you in just now. The caller wouldn't give their name and insisted the call was private. I do know it was a woman.'

Gale and I exchanged glances. I could feel his excitement building.

'Robert took the call. I gather from Felicity it went on for some time. Immediately following it, he came to see me and requested three weeks off. He wouldn't say what it was about and I didn't pry. He left Felicity the post office at Lower Bramsham as a forwarding address for any ongoing mail, and expressly requested that no one from this firm try to contact him directly.'

'You have no idea what business he was about?' Gale asked.

'None! But if I did, I wouldn't discuss it with you. How long do you imagine our firm would continue in existence if we discussed our clients' private investigations with the first people who walked into my office?' He looked at me pointedly. 'Your father would understand,

and wouldn't expect me to betray confidences. I can tell you that Robert was one of one our best investigators. He blended in — always managed to convey a nondescript personality as a front, though beneath that he was as sharp as a razor, like a hunting dog on the scent. And to be murdered in this horrible way, he must have discovered something that involved the gravest issues and a powerful motive.' He put his head in his hands. 'My worst fears have been realised. Forgive me, gentlemen . . . I am not myself today.'

Simon Gale reached forward, and with humility I didn't think he possessed, waited patiently until James Lawson recovered sufficiently to look up. Looking him in the eye, Gale said: 'Will you work with me to find the killer of your nephew, Mr. Lawson? I give you my word that I'll leave no stone unturned until I bring him to justice.'

James Lawson looked bewildered at this pledge. 'I would willingly work with you Mr. Gale, but I have no idea who you are.'

For once I saw Simon Gale at a complete loss. He turned to me and said: 'Tell him everything.'

* * *

As we emerged from 16a Gilder's Court, Gale headed as if by instinct for a pub called The White Swan. He paused outside. 'This is what I need,' he said as he pulled me inside. 'Beer!'

I had done my best to introduce Gale to James Lawson and give him credibility, as well as describe the events from the dinner last Friday at Hunter's Meadow, to our arrival at Fetter Lane. He had listened without a word of interruption, making a few notes on a pad. No doubt, as soon as we had left, he would instigate his own investigation.

Gale and I both agreed Lawson knew more than he was letting on. He knew for what purpose his nephew Robert Lawson, masquerading as William Baker, had gone to reside incognito at Lower Bramsham for three weeks. After all, what was the regular mail from the London office to

Lower Bramsham, if it wasn't the fruits of some sort of investigation Baker was working on? We had come away with only one real lead: a woman had made the initial call, and had been put through to Baker — I still had to think of him with that name; and he had respected or known the caller well enough to engage in a lengthy conversation and respond with immediate action.

'If you were going to employ a private detective, would you want anyone to know about it?' said Gale as he guzzled his first pint. 'He'd made up his mind by the end of the conversation to go straight away to Lower Bramsham. The woman on the other end of that telephone had a powerful control over him. I'd give my eye teeth to know who it was. Who d'you think, hey? The attractive Mrs. King, the curvaceous Mrs. Hope, the beautiful Ursula? Or, perhaps you prefer the delicate Agnes Beaver, or ... ' He cocked one eyebrow. ' ... the impish Zoe?'

'That's ridiculous,' I said, feeling outraged. 'How could Zoe have had anything to do with it? She wasn't there at the dinner, and arrived after Baker had vanished.'

'Did she?' demanded Gale, delighted he'd got under my skin. 'How do you know? Oh, I agree it seems that way, and she's likeable enough.'

'Don't be absurd,' I retorted angrily.

'Absurd — ridiculous?' He snapped his fingers and scowled. 'They're not *reasons*. She could've arrived earlier; she could've engaged Baker for some purpose of her own. Maybe that was the real reason she came to Lower Bramsham.'

'You know very well she came to visit Ursula,' I broke in. 'You know that perfectly well.'

'I only know that's *what she said*,' he emphasised, summoning a kindly expression. 'It might've just been an excuse.' He saw the expression of anger on my face and went on quickly: 'Oh, I know you like the woman. But see reason, Trueman. We've got to consider every possibility, d'you see?'

'I can't think of a single logical reason why Zoe would engage Baker to go to

Lower Bramsham,' I argued, feeling myself flush red.

'Of course you can't. That's why it's a mystery.' He finished his beer and ordered another. 'We'll concentrate instead on thimbles, forks, railway-shares and soap!' he said with a gleam in his eye and a hint of wickedness. 'That's the proper and recognised formula for hunting a Snark!'

I stared at him. Was he playing with me? Did he know Zoe Anderson's family business was soap?

$\star$ $\star$ $\star$

We caught the three fifty-six to Marling Junction, and during the journey Gale hunched himself up in a corner of the compartment and only moved to roll an occasional cigarette. It was raining when we arrived back; a thin, cold, wetting drizzle. As we came out of the station, we ran into Agnes Beaver. She looked very fragile and delicate in a mackintosh with a hood that covered her silver hair.

'Have you just arrived on the London train?' she asked when we had exchanged the usual greetings. 'I've been shopping — just a few things for my lacework. If I'd known the weather was going to turn out like this, I'd have postponed it. Are you on your way to Lower Bramsham?'

'Yes,' answered Gale. 'We shall have to organise a car.'

'I have my own little car just round the corner,' said Miss Beaver. She looked at Gale a little doubtfully. 'Mind you, it's very small and you might find it a squeeze, but . . . '

'That's very kind of you,' broke in Gale with alacrity.

She led the way round by the side of the station entrance to a small car park. The car was very small and very ancient, but we somehow managed to wedge ourselves in by redistributing Miss Beaver's parcels.

Agnes Beaver was a careful driver. It may have been that the car was incapable of greater speed, but we never exceeded twenty miles an hour throughout the journey. As we came to the outskirts of

Lower Bramsham eventually, Miss Beaver suggested we might like to have some tea with her. 'I have some homemade scones and jam,' she said persuasively.

I wasn't too enthusiastic about this idea, as I was beginning to worry about my absence from Hunter's Meadow and old Bellman's acquisition. However, Gale accepted her invitation instantly, so there wasn't much I could do about it. I realised, of course, that her invitation provided the perfect opportunity to find out more about one of the dinner guests and see if she had any motive for employing William Baker.

We turned off into a pretty little lane and arrived outside a charming cottage cheered up with Michaelmas daises and chrysanthemums. The interior was neat and not overly cluttered. I had expected the place to be littered with specimens of Miss Beaver's hobby, but with the exception of a single exquisite lace runner on a side table there was no sign of it.

'Please make yourselves comfortable while I get the tea ready. Can I ask you not to smoke? The pollution, you know.'

I grinned at Gale, who sat in a chair while I took the settee. He suddenly looked petulant, like a little boy refused sweets. 'Not the kind of person likely to employ a private detective,' I whispered maliciously.

Gale leaned forward. 'That's where you're wrong,' he retorted irritably. 'Completely, utterly, and absolutely wrong! If it was the only way to attain a desired objective, there would be no hesitation. The whole thing would be considered calmly and dispassionately, d'you see?'

'I don't see,' I argued. 'In my opinion you've picked the two most unlikely candidates to have a reason for consulting Baker — Zoe and Agnes Beaver!'

'I haven't picked anybody,' answered Gale. 'I agree neither is likely, but you can't wash them out for that reason.'

'The obvious candidate is Bellman,' I asserted. 'Occam's razor — the simplest reason is usually the correct one.'

'All served up on a plate, eh? The eternal triangle — husband, wife and another man. What about Gifford? He

180

could be the hub of this whole business — in which case neatness and tidiness go out the window.' He got up and stood by the window, glowering out into the wet garden and tugging irritably at his beard. 'What was the reason for Baker coming to Lower Bramsham? Was he murdered because of that, or because he stumbled on something else?'

'Well if it was because he stumbled on something else accidentally, it's not going to help us much if we do discover his original purpose, is it?' I reasoned.

'If he discovered something accidentally, it's going to be a mighty head-cracker to find out what it was,' he confessed, crossing from the window over to stare at a glass display cabinet. 'Do you see this?' he said excitedly, ruffling his hands through his hair. 'A collection of old English thimbles!'

Before I could express my astonishment, Miss Beaver came in with a lovely old Georgian tray that looked to be solid silver, with a beautiful Rockingham china service. 'Do you both take milk and sugar?'

When she had poured out the tea and we had helped ourselves to buttered scones and jam, she said: 'I find it terrifying that anyone in Lower Bramsham could be capable of these terrible crimes. Who'd want to kill Franklin Gifford?' She considered her own question for a few moments. 'Actually, I can think of several people!'

Gale and I sat up as if given an electric shock.

She shook her head sadly. 'Mr. Gifford used to live at Marling with his wife, Mary. He was the manager of a large bank then. As a bank manager he was quite ruthless; refused help to several people I know. People he turned down for no good reason. People with assets. A nice house he had there in Marling. He had assets.' She suddenly turned quite spiteful. 'I never liked him and I never trusted him.'

'You knew him quite well then, eh?' asked Gale.

She nodded. 'He was in the war.'

'That's interesting,' murmured Gale. He stuffed a whole scone into his mouth, much to my horror. 'I didn't know that.'

'Oh yes. Wounded in the head. Quite badly injured, he was. It was while he was convalescing at a requisitioned country house outside Marling that he met his wife. She was a nurse. Mary was a lovely woman. I watched her fall for him.'

'You were there?' Gale coaxed her on.

'Oh yes. I was the matron. I didn't like him, and advised her against the marriage. He was only interested in himself.'

'What happened to his wife?'

'She died about three years ago.'

'I'm sorry to hear that,' answered Gale, not at all sorry. This was what he was after — background information, better collected in his opinion without officialdom. 'What happened?' he asked.

'Well, it's generally thought she committed suicide.' Agnes Beaver slapped her thin bony hands together. 'But she didn't! She may have swallowed some pills, but Franklin Gifford was the reason she took them!'

Gale leaned forward in a conspiratorial manner. 'Why?'

'He was a philanderer, always having

affairs with someone or other. He met these women at the bank — *they* got the loans they wanted, assets or no assets, and often got Gifford as well! He broke her heart and his son's — they don't get on. Young Michael was devastated, and blames his father for his mother's death. He's in the RAF.'

'Ah, his son.' Gale raised one shaggy eyebrow and cocked an enquiring glance at her. 'Do you know any reason why Gifford would want to draft a new will?'

A flash of alarm went across her faded grey eyes. 'I'm sure I don't.'

We both noticed that moment of alarm. *I'm sure you do*, I thought, and I could see Gale thought the same.

'I'm sure his son will inherit,' she said. 'Franklin's supposed to be quite wealthy.'

Gale nodded. 'I'd heard that,' he said, with a glance in my direction.

'When his wife died, he sold up and came to live here above the bank. I mean, we hardly need a bank in Lower Bramsham, do we?'

There was a few moments' silence until Gale dropped his little bombshell: 'Did you know William Baker was a private detective?'

Agnes Beaver, in the act of transferring a portion of scone from the plate to her mouth, suddenly stopped, holding it poised in mid-air, and her faded grey eyes opened very wide as she stared at Gale with a blank expression. Too blank, I thought.

'He was a detective?' she asked innocently, placing the piece of scone carefully back on her plate. 'What was he doing in Lower Bramsham?'

'We don't know,' answered Gale. 'Only that the person who hired him was most likely a woman.'

'Why do you say that?' she asked with a troubled expression.

Rather unwisely, I thought, Gale told her. I was sure Chief Detective Inspector Halliday would strongly disapprove of this wholesale scattering of information. But if such a thing had crossed Gale's mind, he ignored it.

Miss Beaver's troubled expression had faded completely when Gale finished recounting our adventures. 'What a pity after all that trouble you didn't learn more,' she said.

'We collect trifles, hey?' grunted Gale. 'But, d'you see, when you've collected enough trifles you can build up quite a large picture. You've lived here quite a long time?'

Miss Beaver looked a little bewildered at the abruptness of the question. She wasn't used to Gale's habit of suddenly going off on a tangent. 'Nearly sixteen years,' she answered, sipping her tea. 'I was here long before most of our small community.'

'That's what I thought.' Gale leaned forward and ungraciously grabbed the last scone. 'Of all the people at that fateful dinner, who do you think 'ud be the most likely to engage the services of a private detective, and why?'

I formed a picture in my eyes as clear in memory as it had been in reality: old Bellman at the head of the table, peeling a peach; Ursula, facing her husband, her lovely face expressionless; Lance Weston, dark and supercilious, gently twisting the stem of his wine glass; Arnold Hope, fat and shiny, droning on huskily about that interminable shares story; Mrs. Hope, bulging out of that revolting dress; Franklin Gifford, neat and dapper; Agnes Beaver, delicate as a piece of her own china, with a hint of sadness in the depths of those gentle eyes; Edward Cranston, heavy-jawed and pompous; Mrs. Hilary King, vivid and colourful; Jack Merridew, owlish and lantern-jawed. And of course, William Baker — Robert Lawson as we now knew him to be — acting nondescript and nervous while all the while on a mission; an investigation.

The troubled look reinstated itself upon Miss Beaver's features. 'That's a question I'd prefer not to answer, Mr. Gale.'

13

We set off to walk back to Hunter's Meadow. 'I noticed you left your tea,' I mentioned.

'Tea!' Gale repeated, contorting his face into an expression of disgust. 'Hah — water! I never touch the stuff.'

I remarked that for the amount of time we'd spent with Agnes Beaver, we hadn't got very far.

'You don't think so?' Gale gave me a quick sidelong glance. 'We're getting a picture of Franklin Gifford, and it's not so rosy, if everything Agnes Beaver said was true — and we don't have reason to believe it wasn't, hey? Somebody disliked him enough to kill him. Then there's the money, and those successful investments of his. We're led to believe there's a pile of cash sitting somewhere.'

'Probably in his bank,' I ventured, with a smile.

'Probably!' cried Gale. 'Then there's

the small matter of the will — the reason he asked you up to his flat. If he didn't want to leave all his money to his son, what changed his mind? A very important question, this. Who does he now want to leave it to? Did you notice that flash of alarm in Miss Beaver's eyes when I asked her why?'

'I did notice it. You're right,' I conceded, 'we're building up a picture.'

'On the button, young feller — everyone we meet and talk to. That's exactly what we're doing — uncovering the layers; collecting trifles. Then there was that troubled expression of hers when I mentioned it'd been a woman who'd telephoned Baker, and when I asked who she thought would engage a private detective. I'm sure she had a pretty good idea, but she refused to divulge it. Then there was that glass cabinet,' Gale went on, increasing the length of his stride so that I had difficulty keeping pace with him. 'The thimble collection. Isn't that the strangest coincidence? 'They sought it with thimbles,'' he quoted. 'And Agnes Beaver with her thimbles is wittingly or

189

unwittingly helping us hunt the Snark!'

I made up my mind. 'Slow down a moment,' I called to him, so I could speak normally instead of shouting. 'Did you know Zoe's family owns Anderson Soap?'

'I wondered when you were going to tell me,' he growled.

'How did you know?'

'Ursula told me. I think at one time she was a little envious of your Zoe's wealth.'

My Zoe? I smiled to myself. I rather liked the sound of that.

Gale went on: 'Maybe that's one reason she married old Bellman. To even up the score.'

'You don't think there's anything in it do you? 'They charmed it with smiles and soap'?'

Gale roared with laughter. 'Well, young feller, she does have a charming smile and she's got plenty of soap! We'll have to wait and see.'

He picked up the pace again and we lapsed into silence. In spite of Gale's assurances that he would make it all right with Joshua Bellman, I wasn't so convinced. With every yard that brought us nearer to the house I felt guiltier, like a boy skiving off school. We should arrive in time to dress for dinner, and I dreaded the prospect of facing Bellman's shrewd, beady brown eyes. In order to offset this fear I thought of Zoe Anderson. Her presence would more than compensate for any unpleasant remarks Bellman might make. I hope that Ursula had not carted her off anywhere that evening.

I needn't have worried, however, for the first person I saw after Trenton had admitted us was Zoe. She was coming quickly down the wide staircase, and when she saw me she stopped with her hand on the rail and her impish face crinkled into a grin. 'Well!' she said, coming down the remainder of the staircase. 'You've finally come back.'

'Like the prodigal son,' said Gale, stripping off his coat and flinging it at Trenton. 'I'm going up to wash and change. I'm starving. Nothing to eat since breakfast except scones and jam.'

'Dinner will be served in twenty minutes,' murmured Trenton solemnly for anyone who wanted to listen, as Gale bounded up the stairs in great strides, three at a time. 'Drinks are being served in the drawing room.'

'Where have you been all day?' Zoe asked. 'Everyone's been wondering what happened to you.'

My heart sank. 'Bellman?' I asked anxiously.

She nodded.

'Was he annoyed?'

'I don't think so. We haven't seen much of him. Several newspaper reporters have called. They were disappointed that they couldn't see Mr. Gale.'

'Just as well he wasn't here,' I said.

'Where did you go?'

This was awkward. I wasn't at all sure that I ought to tell her — certainly not until I had Gale's permission. She must have seen my uncertainty, for the quirk at the corner of her mouth deepened, and a dancing light of amusement was in her green eyes. 'All right — you needn't answer that. You'd better dress or you'll be late for dinner.'

She turned away with a little wave of her hand and I hurried up the stairs. At the top I almost collided with Joshua Bellman. He looked like a man on the verge of complete nervous exhaustion. His wrinkled face was of an unhealthy pallor and there was a strained expression in his small eyes. He greeted me, however, pleasantly enough, rather to my relief. Apparently he'd seen Gale, who had taken full responsibility for my absence. I started to apologise but Bellman cut me short.

'Don't worry,' he said. 'I've had a telephone call from your father.' He looked at his watch. 'He should be arriving any time soon. We'll both put in a full day tomorrow — so that lets you off the hook to go sleuthing with that maniac Simon.'

It took all my restraint not to jump with joy. I was forced to admit quite candidly to myself that I was far too interested in this Snark business to concentrate on a series of legal clauses and deeds that totally lacked human interest. This was probably not a very promising attitude for a lawyer, and the only excuse I can offer is that close contact with murder changes a person. If they had been straightforward murders, I might not have been affected in the same way and not so intensely interested. My imagination was seething away like a boiling pot and I resented the legitimate reason for being here. I resolved to speak to Gale, who could approach Bellman with a request for me to stay on for a few days. Leaving now to return to London for good would be unbearable. Not just because I wouldn't be able to help Simon hunt the Snark, but I might never see Zoe again.

While I was washing and hurriedly climbing into my dinner suit, I thought I heard a car come up the drive. A few seconds later there was a knocking at the big outer door below and the faint sound of voices.

The dinner gong echoed through the house as I finished dressing and ran down the stairs. There in the hallway shaking hands with Joshua Bellman was my father. I could see at once the chill he had suffered had pulled him down. His face was thinner and his eyes more deeply sunken; there were lines of fatigue running from the corners of his thin lips to the high, curved nostrils and repeated under tired eyes. It was with something of a shock that I realised how old he was looking. It was with relief that I also saw how pleased Joshua Bellman was to see him. I knew I was no substitute for my father's great experience, and I felt inwardly elated that I was now let off the hook.

*   *   *

My father's arrival at Hunter's Meadow had coincided with the almost immediate serving of dinner, and afterwards Bellman monopolised my father for the rest of the evening. Simon Gale, suddenly falling into one of his morose moods, had retired early, barely bothering to wish us goodnight, and I had been dragged into a rubber of bridge with Ursula, Zoe, and Jack Merridew. It was after twelve when we broke up, and by this time Bellman and my father had disappeared, most likely to Bellman's study.

I had a hot bath, got into my pyjamas and dressing gown, and was on the point of going in search of my father when he forestalled me by tapping on the door of my room. It was very late. The big clock in the hall below had faintly struck one some minutes ago, but this was the first opportunity I had of talking to him alone.

'Your letter worried me, Jeff,' he began, stretching out his slippered feet to the electric fire. 'Having seen the headlines on the newsstands — a double murder in this little village, I became even more alarmed. Then yesterday afternoon I had a call from James Lawson, who filled me in on your visit, and I resolved to come down here as soon as possible.'

'James Lawson telephoned you?' I asked in surprise.

'He's done work for me in the past — city fraud, that kind of thing. He's a good man, Jeff, and he was very worried for your safety. That's why I'm really here — so you can return home, and I can finish up this merger for Joshua.'

I couldn't restrain my alarm. 'I have no intention of returning home,' I told him.

'I can't walk out and leave Simon Gale in the lurch. Besides, I — ' I stopped short of blurting out my feelings for Zoe Anderson.

My father gave me stern look. 'I don't think you realise what you've got yourself into, Jeff. This is a very nasty business.'

'I'm aware of that,' I said defensively.

'Lawson thinks so too. You and Simon Gale could be in grave danger if you get too close to this Snark, whoever it is. Do you think they're going to sit and wait until you knock on their door or give the police enough information to catch them? They might come after you.'

'I can take care of myself. I'm not a child any longer.'

'Please don't be silly, Jeff.' My father looked at me in astonishment. 'This is a serious business — a very serious business. You could get killed. And it's not just these murders that worry me — it's this situation between Ursula Bellman and this man, Weston. That's another situation that could explode right in our faces.'

'We don't know the murders aren't

part and parcel of all that,' I replied, and immediately regretted saying it.

'What grounds have you for thinking so?' demanded my father sharply.

I hesitated for a moment, and then told him.

'But there's no actual proof,' said my father cautiously. 'Eye contact between two people, however revealing, is not proof of an affair, as you well know.'

'Zoe Anderson saw it too,' I put in quickly, 'and interpreted it the same way I did.'

'You think the dead man, James Lawson's nephew, may have obtained irrefutable evidence?' He pursed his lips. 'James told me his nephew was here for three weeks but wouldn't go into further detail. Are you telling me that during that time, any agent worth his salt wouldn't have got the evidence of an affair, presented the file and wrapped it up — and the consequences of the whole thing wouldn't have exploded by now? Bellman isn't the type to sit back and do nothing.'

I remembered something Zoe had said to me during our walk back from the village on the day Gale and I visited Weston's cottage. 'This isn't the first time our Ursula has been at this game.' I recounted our conversation.

'It doesn't surprise me,' answered my father. 'She's a stupid, vain, woman. But I don't think she's involved in murder — not just the murder of James's nephew, but this other chap the banker.'

'Franklin Gifford,' I prompted.

'I don't think this possible amorous interlude on the part of Mrs. Bellman has any connection with these dreadful murders. They're of a different order. I urge you again to return home tomorrow.'

★　★　★

I had no intention of returning home. I came down to breakfast ready for battle, and excited to have the day to myself without feeling guilty. I had just poured myself some coffee, and was considering what to eat, when Trenton came in to announce Chief Detective Inspector Halliday was waiting for Gale in the drawing room.

'Come on, young feller,' grunted Gale, swallowing a scalding cup of coffee in one huge gulp, apparently without any ill effects. I grabbed my own coffee, and feeling like an obedient dog, followed my master out of the room.

Halliday was standing in front of the fireplace, staring up at a portrait of Ursula Bellman that hung over the mantelpiece.

'Hello, hello. Damned fine portrait that!' greeted Gale in high good humour.

I looked afresh at the portrait and noticed it was signed 'S. Gale'. If Halliday had noticed, he didn't say anything.

'You're an early bird this morning,' Gale said. 'Looking for worms?'

Halliday turned round and there was a reproachful look in his eyes. 'Good morning, sir. I came early to catch you, in case you had a notion to travel up to London again.'

'Aha!' cried Gale, rubbing his hands together and grinning in huge delight. 'So you know about that, hey?'

'Properly stole a march on us there, didn't you? You took confidential police information and acted on it without proper consultation. The Deputy Chief Constable is none too pleased. The City Police aren't either.'

Gale looked like a little boy who has been scolded for a moment, and then he waved away this mild rebuke. 'Did you get Baker's private address?' he asked eagerly, sidestepping any responsibility.

'Yes we did,' answered Halliday. 'Robert Lawson's private address,' he corrected.

I could see Halliday was dismayed that Gale hadn't taken his gentle warning more seriously, but was unsure how to handle Gale, like many I had met since my arrival in Lower Bramsham.

Gale was rapidly rolling a cigarette from his battered box. 'Where did he live?'

'We got a bit more than that. Mr. James Lawson took us round there and let us in. Very helpful gentleman,' he said pointedly, looking straight at Gale, who was licking down the gummed end of the cigarette paper. 'He lived in one of those small flats off Russell Square.'

'What did you find, hey?' he asked,

striking a match off his thumbnail. 'Don't tell me you found a Mrs. Baker?'

'A Mrs. Lawson, sir. His real name was Lawson.'

'Yes . . . yes!' cried Gale impatiently, lighting his cigarette and drawing in smoke with great enjoyment. He began pacing around the room, puffing so furiously at his cigarette that a little trail of sparks followed him like the tail of a comet. 'You found her?'

'No, sir,' answered Halliday. 'The City Police are carrying out a thorough search as we speak. But there was a marriage certificate. It was dated nineteen thirty-five.' He consulted his notebook. 'The twenty-first of October — and the marriage was between Robert Henry Lawson, described as a lawyer's clerk, and a Miss Hilary Nelson, spinster.'

Gale stopped dead as if he'd walked into an invisible brick wall. He rounded on Halliday ferociously. 'Hilary!'

Into my mind flashed a vision of the dark, pretty woman in the vivid scarlet dress, who had sat next to Arnold Hope at that fateful dinner. Of course there were a lot of Hilarys in the world. The name might only be a coincidence, but . . .

Simon Gale was glaring at Halliday, his beard bristling with excitement. 'Mrs. Hilary King,' he cried. 'Is it too great a leap? By all the buttons on the Pearly King, could it be the same Hilary?'

'It would be a bit of a stretch — ' said Halliday cautiously.

'Let's get our coats,' interrupted Gale, making for the door. 'We'll soon find out!

14

Chief Detective Inspector Halliday drove us into Lower Bramsham. Keeping his eyes on the winding road, he gave a sharp glance at the large figure sitting beside him. 'We heard back from the booking office at Marling Junction. Twenty-five passengers bought tickets, two for Farley Halt — he remembered those because they were unusual on account of it not being very popular. There were two passengers on that last train Monday night who got off at Farley Halt.'

'There we are!' cried Gale, wriggling in his seat with impatience as if he was about to try to stand up. 'That explains it!'

'We visited the man who was on duty at the ticket office that night and showed him a photograph of William Baker we were given by James Lawson. He didn't recognise Baker, or manage a description of the other passenger who purchased a ticket for Farley Halt.' Halliday looked glum. 'Very disappointing.'

Gale didn't look disappointed at all. 'The Snark was on that train. William Baker gets off the train, the Snark follows . . . waits until the train has pulled clear of the station . . . knocks him out . . . strips off his clothes . . . kills him . . . makes certain he's dead, and heaves him through the waiting-room window. He takes Baker's clothes, house key and ticket, puts on Baker's oilskin mackintosh and black-and-white-checked cap, and makes his way to the village. He lets himself into Baker's lodgings, searches Baker's room for any incriminating evidence, and leaves fifteen minutes later, seen by Mr. Freeman. He dumps Baker's clothes, whips off the mackintosh and cap, leaves them on the pavement, and hides until that chap — '

'Mr. Charles Hicknell,' broke in Halliday helpfully.

' — until Hicknell comes along and hears that cackling chuckle. Just before he finds Baker's clothes in a heap.'

We all sat in silence as this action

played through our minds. As vividly as a film on a cinema screen, his words conjured up the damp, misty desolation of Farley Halt, and the murderer struggling to heave that thin body through the waiting-room window.

'I reckon that's just about it, sir,' agreed Halliday, with a smile of satisfaction.

The house occupied by Mrs. Hilary King was situated at the end of a narrow lane running down beside the church, at the top of the high street. It was not very large and of a rather depressing architecture, which I judged to be late Victorian and not in keeping with the rest of Lower Bramwell. There was an outsize conservatory, one of those monstrously ornate domed affairs of glass, built onto the side of the house, which gave it a curious lopsided appearance. The gravel path that ran up to the front door between two oblong strips of grass was dotted with patches of weed, and the flowerbeds looked tangled and neglected. It was quite obvious Mrs. King was no garden-lover.

She answered the door herself in

answer to Halliday's knock. She was dressed in a pair of slim-fitting black slacks and a canary-yellow jumper, which showed to full advantage her admirable figure. Quite understandably, she looked surprised to find three men on her doorstep. I thought I detected a hint of apprehension in her dark eyes at the sight of Halliday and the police car parked outside, but it was gone almost immediately.

'I'm sorry to disturb you, ma'm,' said Halliday, repeating his usual formula. 'I wondered if we could have a word.'

'I've already made a statement, Inspector,' she replied with a puzzled frown. 'I don't know what I could add.'

'Just a word, to save you coming down to the station. Mr. Gale and Mr. Trueman are kindly helping us with our investigation.'

She hesitated for a second while her eyes flickered quickly from one to the other of us. Then she said, with a bright and wholly artificial smile: 'You'd better come in.'

We stepped into a hall that might have

come straight out of *House and Garden*. Everything was immaculate, like a show house, very modern and artistic, but rather sterile. 'You'd better come through to the studio,' she suggested, leading us through a drawing room, through a glass door into the glass conservatory we had seen from the outside.

This was the exact opposite of the rest of the house and looked lived in. There was a large work table littered with head-blocks, buckram shapes, feathers and ribbons, an electric iron, an assortment of scissors, and other paraphernalia required for creating her exclusive model hats. I learned later that these creations were immediately copied in hundreds by a firm for which she worked, and circulated to all the big stores in the country.

She indicated some cane chairs with gaily coloured cushions. 'Please make yourselves comfortable,' she said as she helped herself to a cigarette from a box on the table, inspiring Gale to roll one of his own. 'What is it you gentlemen want to see me about?'

I could tell she was putting on a show and that underneath she was nervous. The flame of the lighter into which she dipped the end of her cigarette wavered from the slight shaking of her hand.

Halliday cleared his throat. 'I'll get straight to the point. I understand you knew Mr. Baker?'

Hilary King shook her head. 'I told you quite clearly before that I didn't,' she replied a little arrogantly.

Halliday smiled and his voice was silky smooth. 'That's quite correct.'

I could see her relief and a return of confidence.

'Would it surprise you to learn that Mr. Baker was a private detective?'

'A detective?' She tried very hard to inject the right element of astonishment into her voice but to my ears it didn't ring true. 'It surprises me very much. I still don't understand how that concerns me.'

Gale lit his cigarette and, drawing the smoke in deeply, leaned forward in expectation, his eyebrows drawn down over his eyes. I knew it didn't ring true to him either.

Halliday's jaw stiffened. The eyes in his round good-humoured face were watchful. He was playing with her like a cat with a mouse. 'Are you a widow, Mrs. King?'

The atmosphere tightened, like over-stretched rope before it frays and snaps. She took a long drag on her cigarette to soothe her obviously quivering nerves and slowly blew out the smoke. Then she seemed to stop breathing. She went very still and seemed to slump. 'Why did you ask me that?' She'd cleverly answered the question with another question.

Gale could restrain himself no longer. 'Murder's a horrible thing,' he said, with an expression on his face that would have scared a hardened commando. 'Especially murder when it's carried out by a perverted joker, with a lot of grotesque trimmings — a joker who planned two diabolical crimes. A joker who first knocked unconscious, then stripped, and then cold-bloodedly thrust a knife through William Baker's skin, into his back.' He smacked his fist into the palm of his hand.

Hilary King visibly flinched, her eyes opened wide, and she grabbed the edge of the work table to steady herself.

Gale continued mercilessly: 'But this won't worry you unduly because you never knew William Baker, did you, Mrs. King?'

Her knuckles were white. I thought perhaps Gale had gone too far and that she might collapse. She swallowed and stifled a sob as she shook her head. The rope was fraying.

Halliday sensed his moment perfectly. In a clear and gentle voice he said: 'Perhaps you knew him as Mr. Robert Lawson?'

I was watching Gale, who was watching her intently; and while she managed a superb job of controlling her emotions, we knew all pretence was over, and we had found Hilary Nelson. Halliday might have struck her a physical blow. She shrank back against a cabinet, groping with her hand to steady herself — and the rope snapped.

'Get out!' she breathed tremulously. 'Get out of my house!'

We had no choice but to leave her alone, still supporting herself by the edge of the work table as if she would collapse at any moment, her face drawn and suddenly haggard, tears beginning to run down her cheeks. I remembered her face in the crowd outside Gifford's flat — she'd looked like that then.

'I don't think there's any doubt that's our Hilary,' remarked Halliday as we made our way back to the police car. 'But was she the woman who rang up the office — the personal caller?'

'Why is she called King?' asked Gale, climbing into the car. 'And why did the Nelson-Lawson marriage break up for some reason or other? They were obviously living apart.'

'I'm expecting a call from the City of London police with the results of searching Robert Lawson's flat,' Halliday told him, climbing in behind the wheel. 'I'll also be speaking to James Lawson. I'll ask him for some family history. The investigation into Franklin Gifford's financial affairs should turn up something very soon. Would you like to come back to my office?'

'Try and stop me!' cried Gale.

★   ★   ★

It was still only just after eleven o'clock that morning when we got to the police station at Marling. Gale went at the problem full throttle:

'We've got two reasons why someone should want to get rid of Gifford. Revenge for the way he treated his wife. His son perhaps hated him — they didn't get along — but a lot of people don't get along and don't murder one another! The other is something to do with the bank — a case of fraud — could be a dozen different things. But what is the connecting link between Gifford and Baker, eh? Baker was killed first, out of sequence, if Lewis Carroll's Snark verses are adhered to. What's the single overriding motive that links these two murders? Now make no mistake, this motive was forming in the mind of the murderer long before that Friday dinner when I dropped my resounding clanger.

Bubbling and festering in his mind, and powerful enough to drive him towards madness. I only provided him with the setting, d'you see?'

'Remind me why he needed a setting?' asked Halliday. 'Why did he need all these theatrics?'

'That's a jackpot question. The method dazzles us, the sleight of hand — and that's the point! It's all designed to sensationalise, to mask a simple plan to murder one person, Franklin Gifford. Baker was killed because he got in the way. During his three weeks poking about, did he discover his wife was living in the village, or did he know it all along? Did he stumble upon Bellman, who had just injured himself, or was that Bellman's excuse for inviting him to dinner — for getting him to Hunter's Meadow to meet the other dinner guests?'

'It covers a clandestine meeting in the woods to discuss the real reason Baker had come to the village,' I suggested.

Gale nodded. 'Bellman knew, through his friendship with Hilary, that she'd been married to a private investigator, so it wouldn't be unnatural to ask her to telephone and arrange for him to come down here. Hilary didn't have to know the real reason she was calling him — and I don't think that reason was the Ursula and Weston relationship — I don't believe that has anything to do with the murders, though it's a tempting solution. Something else; maybe this acquisition you're working on, or something that goes a long way back to the founding of his business empire — a fraud, a double-cross that someone knows about, blackmail — and Bellman wants Baker to investigate; find out who it is. But they're on to him, and they quickly put a stop to it!' Gale glared at us. 'Enter the Snark and exit Baker!'

I tried to work this out. 'Suppose Gifford was the one who was blackmailing Bellman, and Gifford found out Baker was investigating him — then Gifford had a motive to kill Baker.'

'That's right,' agreed Gale.

'But then who killed Gifford?' I asked. 'Bellman?'

Gale ran his fingers through his thick chestnut-red hair until it stood up from

215

his head like Shock-headed Peter, or *Struwwelpeter*, that German book of poems that terrified me as a child.

'That would mean two Snarks,' commented Halliday wryly.

Gale roared with laughter. ''Distinguishing those that have feathers, and bite, from those that have whiskers, and scratch',' he quoted.

A package arrived from the City of London Police that provided us with some interesting information. There was a report on their search of Robert Lawson's home, and a sepia photograph of him with his wife. It was faded, but there was no doubt it was Hilary King.

'I'll apply for an arrest warrant,' stated Halliday angrily. 'I'm going to get her in for questioning, with the strong possibility she will be charged with withholding information from the police and perverting the course of justice.'

'That should open her up like a can of beans,' growled Gale.

A long telephone conversation with James Lawson added to Mrs. Hilary King's history. Apparently after two years of marriage to Robert, she had begun an affair with a buyer at Selfridges, a Mr. Ross King, which resulted in her leaving her husband and going to live with him. James said his nephew was heartbroken, always hoping that she would return to him. Despite protestations from the family, Robert told everyone he would forgive her. Then fate took a hand and King died suddenly. The tables were turned, and heartbroken herself, she went to live alone at lower Bramsham, calling herself Mrs. Hilary King, though they were never married.

'So a telephone call to Robert Lawson would have brought him running, hey?' grunted Gale, frowning. 'Having told everyone she was Mrs. King — wishful thinking, I suppose, as she couldn't have him near the place, or wouldn't — he was forced to keep his distance lodging with Mrs. Tickford and posing as William Baker.'

Sergeant Lockyer came into the office and handed Halliday a report. He opened the file and looked up. 'The investigation into Franklin Gifford's financial affairs. Preliminary results.' After flicking through pages with nothing but columns of figures, he reached a summary page. He looked up with an intake of breath. 'It appears Mr. Gifford died a rich man. Let me see. In various accounts, a total of over twenty thousand pounds!'

'Enough to kill for?' I asked.

'A bit obvious if you're the son and you inherit the lot!' growled Gale. 'I presume his son does inherit?'

'I'll look into that,' promised Halliday.

I thought of Franklin Gifford's desire to draft a new will and considered that for whoever did inherit under the terms of the original will, the timing was very fortunate. A few days later and it might all have changed. The beneficiary under the proposed new will had lost out. I wondered who it was, and reminded Gale and Halliday of this fact, but they had not forgotten.

'If he's a philanderer, the proposed new will might have favoured whoever he might be philandering with, d'you see?' Gale suggested. 'I think we need to be certain who that person is — though I have an idea who it might be.'

Chief Detective Inspector Halliday had an appointment with the deputy chief constable after lunch, followed by a press conference. He offered to drive us back to Hunter's Meadow — I think as a measure to prevent Gale from meeting Major Wintringham-Smythe so soon after our visit to St. Dunstan Investigations. Gale accepted his offer of a lift with alacrity, though I would have preferred to walk. None of us were particularly cheerful. Gale was suffering from a kind of irritable frustration, and even Halliday's usually genial expression was worried and gloomy.

As we approached the Golden Crust, Gale came alive and signalled frantically for Halliday to stop. 'I need beer!' he cried, opening the car door almost before the vehicle had come to a standstill, he was in such a hurry. 'And lots of it! Are you coming, Halliday?'

'No thank you, sir,' answered Halliday, smiling. 'I have to get back.'

'Thank you for the lift. We can walk home from here,' I said as Gale disappeared through the door of the pub.

'Beatrice!' Gale greeted the bar lady

like a long-lost love. 'Beer, and lots of it!'

'Hello, Mr. Gale,' greeted Beatrice, grabbing a tankard.

Gale shook his head and indicated a larger one at the end of the row. 'That's the one — two pints, d'you see? Then I needn't bother you so often! And something for you, Beatrice?'

'Well, that's very kind of you Mr. Gale. I'll just have a small port.'

'Right you are!' Gale cried, his mood considerably improved from when he'd been in the car. Beatrice put our drinks on the bar and Gale took an enormous draft, smacked his lips and cried: 'Beatrice the beautiful.' He beckoned her close.

'Yes, Mr. Gale?'

'I need your help, d'you see?'

Beatrice didn't know if Gale was being serious or having a joke. 'Oh, yes!' she giggled.

Gale beckoned her closer and cocked an eyebrow. 'I need to ask you something I'm sure you will know the answer to,' he whispered conspiratorially. 'It's very important.'

Beatrice flushed and gave him a big grin. 'Oh, all right. I'll do my best.'

'Mr. Gifford.'

Beatrice opened her eyes until they were like saucers.

'Mr. Gifford and Mrs. Hilary King. Was there anything in the nature of an engagement?'

Beatrice looked relieved she hadn't been asked something she couldn't answer. 'There was no engagement or anything like that; just gossip — but everyone knew which way the wind was blowing.'

Gale gave me an exultant look of triumph.

She shook her head sorrowfully. 'It must have been a shock for her, Mr. Gifford, being found like . . . well, you know.'

'I'm sure it was,' agreed Gale. 'I'm sure it was a very great shock.' He turned to me when Beatrice was out of earshot. 'That's the real reason Hilary didn't want her husband too close — it'd blow her relationship with Gifford sky-high. Gradually the picture buried beneath emerges, eh, young feller? Like one painting hidden beneath another.'

15

The house was deserted when we arrived. My father and Bellman were busy in the study, and Jack Merridew had gone off on his bicycle somewhere on an errand. Ursula had gone to Marling to lunch with some friends and was not expected back until late in the afternoon. There was no sign of Zoe Anderson anywhere, and according to Trenton she had not gone with Ursula.

Simon Gale went straight to his room to think, he said, and so I was left to my own devices. I wandered restlessly into the empty dining room; the long table was already set for luncheon. I opened one of the windows and stepped out onto the stone-flagged terrace. There was a smell of wet earth and rotting leaves; and across the wide stretch of grass, beyond a ragged line of shrubbery, a thin spiral of smoke was rising. The air was dampish from the rain-soaked ground, but I found it refreshing; and leaning on the broad top of the terrace wall, I lit a cigarette and tried to sort out my impressions of the morning and the revelations concerning Hilary.

It was ridiculous to suppose that she could have anything to do with the murders. If Gifford was in love with her and planning to change his will in her favour, which was the only explanation I could think of, then assuming she didn't reciprocate that love and had other plans, killing him would have cost her a great deal of money and achieved nothing.

I heard a step behind me on the stone paving and swung round. It was Zoe. She was wearing the loose, fleecy coat which she had been wearing when I had first seen her that night in the Golden Crust — the night when Lance Weston's entrance had heralded the recent dreadful events.

'Hello,' she said. 'I hope I didn't startle you? I've been for a walk around the grounds. This is a lovely place, isn't it?'

'I'm afraid I haven't seen much of it,' I confessed.

Her face puckered into a smile and her green eyes twinkled mischievously. 'Too busy playing the great detective?' she taunted.

'That's not only unkind but untrue. Watson perhaps.'

She laughed and leaned against the balustrade, her hands thrust deeply into the pockets of her coat. 'Have you discovered anything? Are the police any nearer to capturing this maniac?'

'You think a maniac is responsible?'

Her thin eyebrows curved upwards in surprise. 'Don't you?'

'I honestly don't know what to think any longer,' I answered, not wishing to start any controversy.

'Well, I refuse to believe anyone sane could have carried out those horrible crimes. The terrifying possibility, truly terrifying, is that it might be someone we've met.'

'Let's not talk about it,' I said. 'I'm going to suggest that we go for a long walk this afternoon and leave all the spooks and horrors behind us. Perhaps we could have tea somewhere.'

'I'd like that,' she broke in impulsively, her eyes sparkling.

'That's settled, then. We'll go immediately after lunch,' I declared.

★ ★ ★

I have a most vivid recollection of that afternoon with Zoe among the lanes and woods of Lower Bramsham because it marked a wonderful interlude before once again we were to be terrorised by the Snark.

Lunch was not a long meal that day. My father and old Bellman were obviously anxious to get back to work on the acquisition, while Gale, unusually silent and scowling at his plate, ate practically nothing. Jack Merridew didn't put in an appearance at all — presumably he was still engaged on whatever business had taken him out — so that there were only five of us grouped round one end of the long dining table.

While I was in my room, I heard an appalling din from the direction of the garage and recognised the sound of that fiendish contraption that Simon Gale called a motorcycle. With a noise like a miniature air raid, it popped and banged and exploded past the house, and it was not until it had receded into the distance that tranquillity was regained. Gale had evidentially gone off somewhere on his own, and not, as I concluded from his behaviour at lunch, in a particularly good mood.

Zoe and I left Hunter's Meadow just after two o'clock. I hoped that it would keep fine. There was a mackerel sky of white cloud. It was quite warm, and although there was a slight breeze, it wasn't strong enough for real discomfort.

We elected to leave the village behind us and set off in the opposite direction when we turned out of the drive. I had never chosen this way before and neither had Zoe. The road wound pleasantly between steep banks of moss and grass, topped by a forest of trees whose branches met overhead, forming an interlaced tracery against the sky. We walked down this autumnal tunnel, feeling secure and protected, until after a while we came out into the open again and began to climb steeply. The trees thinned out and eventually frayed away altogether, giving way to low-growing woody vegetation, as the road widened out and merged with a wide expanse of gorse-dotted common land. This was Bramsham Heath, an uncultivated wilderness.

Close to where the road had emerged was a narrow path that ran back along the fringe of a dense wood. We decided this looked more attractive than the common that stretched before us, exposed and windswept as it was, and covered with hummocks of coarse grass. It looked as if walking might be difficult.

Zoe hadn't said very much since we left Hunter's Meadow, but her impish face was aglow, and every now and again she would glance up sideways at me with one of her attractive crinkly smiles, and I knew she was enjoying herself.

For two and a half hours we rambled through woods and lanes and narrow footpaths, losing all sense of direction, so that we were surprised when we came out onto a bridle path and found ourselves on the outskirts of the village. When we had turned back upon reaching Bramsham Heath along by the wood, we had begun walking in a circle. After this long walk we were thirsty and sprinted the last few steps to the teashop.

Being alone with Zoe for so long, at ease with each other, and experiencing such a wonderful afternoon . . . well, I couldn't remember ever feeling as good as this, and I told her.

'I'm sorry it's nearly over,' she said. 'There's a sort of magical spell about the country — the real country where there's nothing but trees and grass and fields. You know what I mean, don't you?'

'It's fantastic,' I said, taking her hand.

Out in those thick and silent woods and winding lanes, far from civilisation, with only the occasional flutter and twitter of a bird to break the pervading stillness — peace could be found there; sanctuary from the stress of life; a natural catharsis that purged the soul.

We had almost reached the entrance to Goose Lane when Zoe suddenly stopped, let go of my hand and grabbed me by the arm. I wondered what had happened for a moment, and then following the direction of her eyes, I saw.

The front door of Lance Weston's cottage had opened and Ursula Bellman was coming out. She moved swiftly and rather furtively down the little path, stepped quickly out the gate, and hurried away in the direction of the high street. She hadn't seen us. We were further down on the opposite side of the road.

'Whose house was that?' whispered Zoe, looking up at me.

I told her and her forehead puckered up in a worried frown.

'So that's where she really went,' she said in a hurt voice. 'That settles any speculation, doesn't it? I mean, lunch in Marling — a deliberate lie. What a fool she is!' Zoe looked worried and a little tearful. 'I have to stop her before Mr. Bellman finds out and it's all over.'

'It's a difficult situation,' I agreed.

Zoe went on: 'I thought all this nonsense would be over when she decided to marry Mr. Bellman.' She stared at me, obviously trying to make up her mind about something. 'Let's go and have some tea.' She took my arm. 'I want to tell you something I've never told anyone else.'

The little teashop was empty, and we took off our coats and settled ourselves at a corner table. When the elderly woman, whom I suspected was not only the waitress but the owner, had taken my order and departed, I leaned forward towards Zoe conspiratorially. 'You're going to tell me that this isn't the first time Ursula has been up to fun and games,' I said.

Her green eyes widened. 'How did you know?'

'You hinted something of the kind the other day. I gathered it was something that happened while you and she were sharing the flat together.'

She rested her elbows on the table. 'Ursula is an orphan, you know. Both her parents were killed in an accident when she was three years old. She was brought up by her grandmother, and after she died, by an aunt who was very strict. She never said anything definite to me about it, but I could see by the expression on her face that she was abused. I know she didn't have a happy childhood — she told me she was unhappy and miserable. She was never allowed any sort of freedom — dances, boyfriends, all the things that most women have.'

I wondered if Zoe had a boyfriend. It hadn't occurred to me until now. I really didn't know much about her, and resolved to find out more. I cut short my thoughts to concentrate on what she was telling me.

'I'm telling you this because I believe it was partly the reason that when she did get free — ' She broke off as the elderly woman appeared with our tea. When she had set it down on the table and gone, Zoe continued: 'Ursula loves to be admired. Oh I know, most women do, but with Ursula it's a kind of desperate necessity. She was only really happy when she was surrounded by a circle of men, and of course with her looks she had no trouble attracting them.'

She poured out the tea while she

continued talking. 'I suppose I must shoulder some of the blame for what happened,' she went on, helping herself to a muffin. 'Knowing what she was like, I ought to have taken better care of her. But I couldn't go everywhere with her, could I? The truth is if I had, she would've resented my intrusion, and that would've been the end of our friendship.'

'What happened?' I asked.

'It was a man she got mixed up with when she went to Monte Carlo on a modelling job at the Hotel de Paris.' She hesitated, but I guessed what was coming.

'Do you mean there was a child?' I asked bluntly.

She nodded. 'Yes.'

'What happened to it?'

'Well that's just it . . . ' she began.

I sensed her difficulty in betraying a confidence, but I think she was relieved to tell someone, and I was very glad she had chosen me.

'It was because of the child that I came down here unannounced to see her.'

No wonder I had detected a false note in Ursula's smiling welcome on the night of Zoe's unexpected arrival at Hunter's Meadow. Obviously she had no wish to be reminded of this past indiscretion.

Zoe told me that Ursula, in the natural course of her modelling job, had been sent to Monte Carlo. She'd travelled on the Le Train Bleu. It was the first time she had been abroad, and either the romantic surroundings, or more probably the champagne that seemed to have been the accompaniment of an apparently endless round of parties, had gone to her head. Whatever the actual trigger, she had become tangled up with a man of ill repute who had been staying at the same hotel. It was too late when she found out just what kind of man he was — a gambler with debts piling up, and an aviator mixed up in some shady goings-on.

'An aviator?' I repeated, intrigued. 'He owned his own aircraft?'

'I gather so,' Zoe answered, not really sharing my interest.

I imagined the man as a George Coleman lookalike, and Ursula in a magnificent evening gown meeting him over cocktails somewhere exotic with a backdrop of palm trees and the Mediterranean sparkling in the moonlight. A plane would zoom in low over the water on a secret mission, maybe smuggling in a spy. I saw the man brandishing a revolver.

'It was a very hectic and passionate affair while it lasted,' Zoe was saying, pulling me out of my imagined scenario and back to the reality of the teashop with a jolt. 'The aftermath of it was disastrous!'

Zoe had known nothing about it until several weeks after Ursula had returned home. Then she had noticed that Ursula was worried about something, but she never dreamt what it was until one night when Ursula broke down, had a fit of hysterics, and sobbed out the truth on her friend's shoulder.

'She was frantic with worry,' said Zoe, her green eyes clouding at the recollection. 'She'd taken all sorts of crazy things in an attempt to . . . well, none had any effect except to make her feel ill. She was at her wits' end and terrified that anyone should know.'

'What happened to the child?' I asked.

'I took care of that,' she answered. 'I sent her away to my sister Lucy, who lives in the country. Her husband owns a small farm. The baby was born there. There were complications. Ursula can't have any more children.'

'Is the child still living with your sister and her husband?'

'I was a fool to think — and so was Ursula — that you could just dump a baby on someone and all your troubles would go away. You see, a fresh difficulty has cropped up.'

'Your sister doesn't want to keep the baby any longer?' I cut in, hazarding a guess.

She shook her head. 'I am afraid it's the exact opposite! They want to adopt him legally.'

'How old is he?'

'He's name is Peter and he's nearly seven. He's the cutest little boy. He thinks of Lucy and Andrew as his real mother and father.'

'A legal adoption shouldn't be difficult,' I said, trying to be helpful. 'There are several formalities to be complied with, of course. An application has to be made to the court, and Ursula will have to sign her consent to the adoption and agree to renounce absolutely and unconditionally any control or rights to the child.'

'She refused to do anything,' Zoe interrupted.

'Did she explain why?'

She shook her head. 'No, she wouldn't. That's the trouble. That's why I'm here.'

We both needed a short break from this discussion, which was obviously distressing Zoe. I took the opportunity to eat a muffin while I considered what could be done, while she poured some more tea.

I tried to think of reasons why Ursula wouldn't want to provide Peter with a secure future. Maybe because she was orphaned at three years old, she felt that by signing the forms she was making Peter an orphan as well. Maybe she had discussed the whole thing with her husband and they were looking to adopt. Or maybe she still had feelings for the father. I'd gone quiet while I was trying these possibilities out in my mind, and Zoe was obviously embarrassed she had involved me in something that was really none of my business.

'I'm sorry if I've spoilt the afternoon by bringing all this up,' she began apologetically with a frown, after staring meditatively out of the window for a while.

'Nonsense!' I replied quickly. 'I'd like to help.'

There was another short silence while she looked at me appealingly. 'You're a kind man, Jeff — may I call you that?'

I could feel myself flush, delighted beyond words that this confidential conversation had deepened the relationship between us. 'Of course, Zoe. I'd like you to.'

'I thought she'd learned a lesson,' she said with a bitter smile. 'But now Ursula's starting all over again with this man, Weston. What can we do?'

This put me in some difficulty. I noted she used the word *we*, and was pleased to be included, but there wasn't anything much anybody could do. The only person who could put this situation right was Ursula herself.

Zoe looked up suddenly, her frown vanishing as her face crinkled into one of her impish and attractive smiles. 'It's really not your problem.'

'Have you said anything to Ursula about Weston?'

'What's the use? Until today I hadn't absolute confirmation.'

'Do you mind if I tell my father about the child? He already knows about Weston.'

'What did he say?' she asked quickly.

I repeated, as near as I could remember, the conversation I'd had with my father last night. 'He won't do anything that's likely to precipitate any trouble,' I concluded, 'but just in case things do blow up, it would be a good thing to put him completely in the picture.'

Rather reluctantly, I thought, Zoe agreed. I spent a few minutes persuading her that my father and I would keep everything she had told us confidential, and that she could rest assured my father would not infringe that confidentiality by mentioning any of it to Joshua Bellman or anyone else.

Just as we were getting up to leave, a police car, its blue light flashing, went by, and I just managed to catch a glimpse of Hilary King — or rather Mrs. Hilary Lawson, as we now knew her — sitting in the back.

*　　*　　*

When we got back to Hunter's Meadow, the house seemed as dead and deserted as when we had left it. The big drawing room was empty. If Ursula had come home after we had seen her leave Lance Weston's cottage, she'd either gone out again or sought the seclusion of her own room. My father, I guessed, was in the study with old Bellman, adding the final touches to the acquisition. What had happened to Simon Gale I had no idea. Most likely he was still out. Zoe and I both decided a clean-up was in order after our long walk, and we retired to our respective rooms.

I couldn't get that fleeting image of Hilary in the back of the police car out of my mind. Obviously Halliday had got his warrant and arrested her. It was the first positive step in this whole affair, and I couldn't help speculating what would become of it. Would she admit to telephoning her husband at St. Dunstan and explain why? I couldn't wait for the outcome.

There was plenty to discuss at pre-dinner drinks in the drawing room. Old Bellman looked very pale and was talking earnestly to my father, who gave me a sharp look of irritation as I came into the room. There was no sign of Simon Gale. Ursula looked beautiful and immaculate as usual, but preoccupied, which didn't surprise me. But Zoe did: the fresh air, a figure-hugging pale green dress, and her hairdo contributed to silence everyone in the room as she entered. She looked radiantly beautiful.

'Good evening, everyone,' she greeted with a sweet smile, turning her green eyes in my direction. 'Things have been happening, I hear.'

Did I notice a flicker of jealousy in Ursula's eyes at Zoe's eye-catching entrance? 'Mrs. Hilary King has been arrested and is at Marling police station,' she answered, giving Zoe a charming smile. 'I expect Mr. Gale is there too, as he finds it impossible to keep his nose out of other people's business.'

I was suddenly glad I was here and not with Gale, or my welcome at Hunter's Meadow might have been cut short in my absence. My work on the acquisition was over.

Zoe saw the worried look on my face and quickly came to my defence. 'Ursula, Mr. Gale is working tirelessly to help the police find this killer, which is surely in everyone's interest, is it not? And surely we should also thank Mr. Trueman for giving up his free time to assist where necessary.'

Ursula's beautifully pencilled brows rose slightly. 'Of course we should, Zoe. I'm sure it's very kind of Mr. Trueman to care so much about our small community.'

She managed to say this without

looking at me, as if I wasn't in the room. At that moment we all paused to listen to the extraordinary, but by now familiar, sounds that were approaching from outside: splutters and bangs, as if a war had broken out. Simon Gale had arrived back on his diabolical machine just in time for dinner.

Gale came into the room like a force of nature, so that I for one took a step back. I noticed that Zoe did to, looking mildly alarmed, bracing herself for bad news, as it was evident from the manic expression on Gale's face that he had something important to tell us.

'Miss Hilary King, under threat of arrest and a night in jail, has broken down and revealed all,' he said dramatically.

I noticed Bellman look up and frown.

'I have just come from Marling police station,' Gale went on, revelling in the knowledge that he held the floor. 'Hilary was not arrested, you will note, only taken in for questioning, and she's now been returned home. I doubt if Halliday will charge her.'

'Have you been at the police station all

afternoon?' I asked accusingly, feeling I had been left out.

Gale waved his arms about in the air and answered in a gruff booming voice: 'No. I spent an illuminating afternoon looking through archives at the *Marling Chronicle*, and called in to see Halliday on my way back.'

The dinner gong rang. Jack Merridew, Bellman's lantern-jawed secretary, entered, and, nervously adjusting the position of the shell-rimmed spectacles on his nose, went over to Bellman and handed him a piece of paper, which he took and read without any reaction except to gently rub his chin.

Despite her previous accusations, Ursula was as interested as the rest of us to hear any latest development in the hunting of the Snark. She turned her pale gold head towards Gale, stared at him with her deep blue eyes, and asked in a soft and clear voice: 'Are you getting anywhere close to discovering who it is?'

'More like who it isn't, hey?' he boomed. 'I'm whittling it down. I'm gathering trifles, painting pictures in my head, and eliminating suspects.' Thrusting forward a bristling and belligerent beard, he added in a menacing growl: 'Then I'll just be left with a Snark!'

Trenton entered to announce that dinner was served. We all filed into the dining room, each in our own way preoccupied with what Gale had just said.

Over a dinner of excellent duck, bit by bit, Gale told Hilary's story, beginning with her marriage to Robert Lawson. The idea of Mr. Robert Lawson and Mrs. Hilary Lawson was something they would only get used to in time. He explained how Hilary had met a Mr. Ross King, a buyer at Selfridges, who had died suddenly following an operation in a London hospital for throat trouble. She had come to live at Lower Bramsham, calling herself Mrs. King, as if refusing to acknowledge her lover's death. Opening an account at the local bank, she had met Franklin Gifford.

'Then we come to the telephone call to St. Dunstan Investigations,' bellowed Gale, shifting his large bulk so that his chair creaked and groaned, and waving his arms about to the immediate danger of Merridew, who sat next to him. 'Hilary admitted it was she who telephoned her husband and got him to come down to Lower Bramsham as William Baker and take lodgings with Mrs. Tickford.'

'Did she explain the reason?' I asked.

'I was the reason!' announced the dry voice of Joshua Bellman, his small brown eyes contracting slightly. 'I asked Hilary to telephone her husband.'

The table fell into silence.

'You, darling?' asked Ursula in a shocked voice. Her face had gone white as a sheet. I could see, as she desperately took a gulp of wine, that her hand holding the stem of the glass was shaking. I looked at Zoe, who was already giving me a warning stare, and I knew we were both bracing ourselves for the same reason. Gale had lit a fuse and we were waiting for the bomb to go off.

'I should've thought it was obvious,' grunted Bellman, his thin lips twisting into a faint smile. 'I wanted him to carry out an investigation for me.'

You could have heard one of Hilary's hatpins drop. Nobody dared to ask what that 'investigation' was, but they were all speculating like crazy. The tension in the room was almost tangible.

Bellman didn't look at all ruffled by these revelations. It seemed to me that he thought the whole matter a gross impertinence, and was almost enjoying himself seeing everyone's discomfort.

I remembered Bellman describing that fortuitous arrival of Baker coming to his aid in the woods when he ostensibly twisted his ankle. It appeared less fortuitous and more of a deliberate meeting. Then there was the afternoon I had off when Bellman went out. Was that another meeting with Baker?

'Do you mean to say this investigation you commissioned led to these two murders?' asked Ursula fearfully.

'I didn't mean to say anything, my dear,' retorted Bellman, with no trace of apology in his small black eyes. 'If I'd meant to say anything, I would've invited Robert Lawson here and announced my intentions to the world, wouldn't I?'

Gale roared with laughter and banged the table, much to everyone's alarm and astonishment. 'By Jove you would, Joshua! By Jove you would!' he thundered.

'It was a few days' work,' explained Bellman, looking at his wife. 'A business matter.'

I could see the blood flow back into Ursula's face. The tension lifted a little, but not totally. I assumed this was because none of us knew what revelation was going to come next.

'Could that business matter have anything to do with his murder?' asked Ursula.

'It may do,' her husband answered cryptically. 'That police chap Halliday is coming here in the morning, and I'll discuss it with him.'

I remembered the slip of paper handed to Bellman by Jack Merridew in the drawing room just before dinner was announced. I assumed that had been about Chief Detective Inspector Halliday calling.

'When did Baker complete his work for you?' asked Gale in a booming voice that immediately placed him at the centre of attention again.

'He'd completed most of it,' answered Bellman. Then he added as an afterthought: 'He was very efficient.'

I looked over at Merridew to see his reaction to this news of an investigation — anything that indicated as Bellman's secretary he might have known about it. But his face was impassive.

'Apparently Baker hoped to persuade his wife Hilary to come back and make a go of it,' Gale said. 'Not realising, of course, that she was seeing Franklin Gifford.' His face contorted into a fierce scowl. 'It's terrible when one person's infatuated but the other doesn't care a jot!'

I wondered if that had ever happened to him. 'Did he know about Gifford?' I asked.

'You mean did Baker know that Franklin Gifford and his wife were having an affair?' answered Gale harshly. 'He might've picked up some gossip or stumbled on something. Maybe he got himself murdered for it.'

'I wonder what Hilary will do now,' said Ursula, smiling sweetly at everyone. 'She's lost her husband and her lover.'

'How very careless of her,' remarked Gale.

★ ★ ★

After dinner, Bellman invited Gale to accompany him to his office. I presumed it was to discuss the meeting with Halliday in the morning. They did not return for the remainder of the evening. I felt further left out as I followed the others into the drawing room for coffee. We listened to a concert on the radio, and, following a short discussion after that, we all drifted off to bed.

No sooner had I entered my bedroom than my father tapped on the door. 'I'm planning to return to London tomorrow,' he told me straightaway, 'and I strongly suggest you do the same.'

I nodded, not wishing to start an argument, and turned on the fire.

'The acquisition documents are completed at last. Mr. Merridew will type them up over the next couple of days in preparation for a meeting of the board next week at Bellman's London offices. Of course, once the plans are ratified, Bellman, who is cash-rich at the moment, will become poorer.'

'A lot of his money will be converted into assets,' I said. 'Substantial ones.'

'Yes indeed,' agreed my father with legal gravitas. 'A large amount of money.'

I had questions I wanted to ask him. To begin, I told him I had seen for myself Ursula leave Weston's cottage. Then I relayed what I had learned from Zoe about Ursula's visit to Monte Carlo and the disastrous aftermath of that visit, the birth of her child Peter. 'Do you know of any reason why Bellman would hire a private detective?' I concluded.

My father sat down and made himself comfortable. 'Bellman's father rented a corner shop,' he began. 'It provided enough money for them to live on, but that's about all. When Joshua was old enough, he began working in his father's shop — learning the ropes, ordering goods, keeping accounts. Joshua never went to college or anything like that. He had a very basic education, preferring to educate himself. He was born shrewd. He was frugal, saving his money until he was able to rent his own shop. His father worked one, he worked the other. By the time he was married, he'd bought his shop and already owned three others, and had bought shares in a pie company — he was their best client. He then opened a wholesale grocery company and began deliveries to schools, restaurants and hotels. He expanded rapidly from there.'

'A self-made man,' I commented.

My father nodded. 'Very much so,' he agreed. 'The marriage provided him with two sons. Unfortunately his wife died giving birth to the second.'

I couldn't help but think of the lines from 'The Hunting of the Snark': *The Bellman himself they all praised to the skies, such a carriage, such ease and such grace! Such solemnity, too! One could see he was wise, the moment one looked in his face!* Was Joshua Bellman the key figure in these events? 'What happened to his sons?' I asked.

'Both killed in the war — in the trenches.'

'That's bad luck,' I said, feeling sorry for Bellman. 'Who inherits the empire?'

'The main beneficiary is Ursula.'

I had assumed this, but to actually hear it spoken aloud caused me to pause and remind myself of the age difference between Ursula and Bellman, and the amount of trust he must have in her. It made her liaison with Lance Weston all the more dangerous, the two of them perhaps wanting a life together that was just out of reach unless Joshua Bellman was removed, as well as anyone else who posed a threat. A motive for two cruel murders, with the possibility of a third — Bellman himself? Cash-rich but soon to become cash-poor. It would be difficult for Ursula to get her hands on the bulk of her husband's cash once the acquisition documents were signed and much of his cash had been used to fund it. It would look very odd if, after Bellman bought the additional stores, she suddenly put them up for sale.

But was this scenario fact or fiction? If

it were true, then was Ursula feeding information through to Weston about our activities? Were they plotting to remove Bellman out of their way permanently?

'You think Ursula and Weston are behind these murders?' asked my father, reading my mind.

'I know Gale isn't keen on the idea,' I admitted, 'but it seems to me a sound explanation — the only one we have right now.'

'Then you think Bellman might be next?' asked my father, looking worried.

'It's logical. Once the acquisition is ratified.'

'Most of his cash will be gone. Of course, it will only be temporary. As the new outlets build profits, his cash pile will go up again, higher and more rapidly than before.'

'The fly in the ointment is the murder of Franklin Gifford,' I said, struggling with the problem. 'We have no explanation for that.'

My father looked at me and hesitated. 'Did you know Franklin Gifford introduced Ursula to Bellman?'

I couldn't hide the shock in my face. 'No, I didn't know.'

Suddenly the murders were linked. Gifford had introduced Ursula to Bellman, who had hired Baker.

'I can see I've surprised you,' he said. 'Wheels within wheels. Bellman and Gifford go back a long way, before our company became involved with his affairs. Before Gifford was a bank manager in Marling, he worked in the city at a merchant bank. He procured money to fund Bellman's ventures, either as loans from the bank or personal investors — he had access to lists. Those who invested in Bellman all got their money repaid, and with interest. But the risks involved at the time were high; and where many banks would have turned Bellman down, Gifford signed off on the loans. He had Bellman where he wanted him; and whereas fees were dutifully paid to the banks involved, additional private fees were paid to Gifford personally.'

I couldn't help but recall the lines from 'The Hunting of the Snark': *But a Banker, engaged at enormous expense, had the whole of their cash in his care.*

'The fact that a well-known bank had come on board,' my father was saying, 'paved the way for Gifford to persuade private investors to chip in — and Gifford was very good at persuading.'

'I take it that you didn't much like Gifford?' I asked.

'I didn't like him, but I didn't have much to do with him. He became less important to Bellman as his enterprises generated sufficient profit to enable Bellman to fund himself without recourse to outsiders. Of course, Gifford didn't like that.' My father's face screwed up in an expression of distaste. 'I suspect Gifford went all out to re-establish his control of some of Bellman's affairs.'

'Are you suggesting blackmail?' I asked, thoroughly intrigued.

'Not exactly blackmail. Bellman would say payment for services rendered.'

'So Gifford ran close to breaking the law.'

'I'd agree with that. He was a rascal beneath a fastidious exterior, and we know he was a serial philanderer.'

'Gifford must've done something to really drive someone wild,' I postulated. 'Something that pushed someone over the edge. Something to do with Hilary Lawson or Bellman or someone else. Something that Robert Lawson stumbled across, that was serious enough to get him killed.'

'You think Gifford was the reason Bellman hired a private detective?' My father pondered this for a moment. 'The moment Robert Lawson was killed, Gifford might have had an inkling why — could even point the finger at who might've done it, so he had to go as well. He confided as much to you didn't he? Occasionally, when an emotionally disturbed person feels threatened and attacked, they may think they need to retaliate — to kill before they are killed. And once a person has killed, they don't have to jump over a hurdle to kill a second time.' He got up. 'Please excuse me, Jeff. It's been a long, complicated day with Bellman, and I'm too tired to think straight.'

My father bid me goodnight and went

to his room. I remained for a few minutes in front of the fire, going over and over possibilities, until I forced myself to stop and got into bed.

I slept fitfully, the following lines going round and round in my head as I tossed and turned: *I engage with the Snark — every night after dark — in a dreamy delirious fight.*

I had no idea that dawn the following day would herald extraordinary events that would bring me face to face with the Snark himself.

PART THREE

The Snark!

For the Snark's a peculiar
creature, that won't
Be caught in a commonplace
way.
Do all that you know, and try all
that you don't:
Not a chance must be wasted
to-day!

'The Hunting of the Snark'
by Lewis Carroll

16

The day began with a frantic knocking upon my bedroom door.

'Who is it?' I mumbled, trying to wake up.

'Get dressed and come downstairs!' Gale's thunderous voice shook the door.

'What is it?' I asked, but he had gone.

I swung my legs out of bed and sat for a moment, wondering what on earth was going on. The room was chilly. It was wet and windy outside, sudden squalls lashing the rain against the window pane. I went over to the wash basin and splashed my face with cold water.

Obviously something serious had happened. I quickly put on my clothes, tore across the landing, and hurried down the stairs. I overtook a gloomy-looking Trenton. His mouth was slack and he was shaking his head in bewilderment.

Gale met me in the hall, his face terrible to behold. 'It's Bellman!'

'What about him?' I asked.

'He's dead!'

I stared at him, thunderstruck. 'Oh Lord! Did anyone hear anything?'

'Apparently not,' answered Gale.

'Where is he?'

'In his bedroom. He's still lying in his bed, knifed in the back like the others.'

I could feel despair wash over me and I struggled to fight it off. This would have far-reaching implications for everyone in the house. 'Where's Zoe?' I asked. 'Is she all right?'

'She's comforting Ursula.'

'How is Ursula?'

Gale made a grim face. 'Distraught. They've sent for her doctor.'

I stood there in front of him, feeling completely helpless, as Trenton reached the hall muttering: 'T-terrible. T-terrible.' He headed off towards the scullery.

Gale followed him with a stare, tugging at his beard. Then he turned his attention to me. 'Can't stand here,' he grunted, taking my arm and dragging me into the front lounge. The little-used room was pleasantly furnished. It was empty and a little chilly.

Gale swiftly closed the door. 'I should've anticipated this,' he growled. 'I didn't think it'd happen so soon. I thought I had more time, d'you see?' He slammed his fist into the palm of his hand. 'I was too slow and terribly wrong!'

'Have you seen my father?' I asked, thinking of the upheaval this would cause.

'Last I saw of him he was in the dining room.'

'Someone's going to have to run things. Bellman's affairs. Ursula.'

Gale gave a dry laugh. 'I doubt if Ursula will be having much to do with anything after this.'

'You think she's involved?'

'If you mean did she plunge a knife in Bellman's back? No, not physically,' Gale said sharply. 'But she has the motive, d'you see? She's the only one, as I understand it, who really benefits.'

I nodded. My father had told me the will was in Ursula's favour, but that information was confidential. I wondered how Gale knew.

He twisted his fingers in his beard

thoughtfully, then said in a low voice: 'There was another of those cards.'

'A card?' I repeated automatically, already knowing what he meant.

He nodded, reciting in the same low tone: ' "The Bellman looked uffish, and wrinkled his brow. 'If only you'd spoken before! It's excessively awkward to mention it now, with the Snark, so to speak, at the door!' " '

'Foolhardy or a lot of nerve,' I commented.

'Incredible nerve! It just might be the undoing of him, eh?'

'Where's the card? Have you got it?'

'I left it for the police exactly as I found it, in Bellman's hand, when I turned back the coverlet.'

'Trenton wouldn't have seen it?'

'He'd have said something if he had,' growled Gale, giving me a sharp look.

'Was it someone in the house?'

'The window by the scullery door was broken. A large stone was used. Paper had been glued with treacle over the glass, so when it was struck it didn't smash all over the floor and wake everyone up. A clever idea. So we're supposed to think the Snark broke in.'

'Supposed? So you do think it was someone inside?'

'It'd be too obvious if there *hadn't* been any sign of a break in, wouldn't it, eh?'

'Halliday was coming this morning to see Bellman,' I reminded him.

'I spoke to him on the telephone just before you came down. Halliday's on his way right now,' said Gale gloomily. 'I ought to have prevented this,' he cried, scolding himself, and obviously furious. 'I should've seen it coming. I *did* see it coming! I should've acted. I was looking for proof, d'you see?'

'What happened when you saw Bellman last night?'

'Bellman was hiding something,' growled Gale.

'I should've thought that was obvious at dinner. What was it he wanted Baker to investigate?'

Gale looked at me. There was a glitter in his eyes, and his beard seemed to quiver with suppressed excitement. 'He said to me: 'Of course I know about Ursula and that chap Weston. I may be an old fool, but I'm not in my dotage. I can't give her what Weston can. What right do I have to take someone as lovely as that and cage them up?''

I stared at him, speechless, for a few moments while I took this in. 'He knew about that? That's a revelation.'

Gale waved a huge arm at me. 'Here's another. It wasn't Ursula and Weston that William Baker came to Lower Bramsham to investigate. Bellman began to take an interest in Ursula's past, and when he spoke to her about it he realised she didn't want to tell him anything. So he spoke to Franklin Gifford, who didn't tell him much either. It was this reluctance that got him intrigued, d'you see?'

'So you know Gifford introduced Ursula to Bellman?'

'Bellman told me last night. He spoke to Hilary King and got himself a private detective. The first nugget of forbidden history Baker dredged up was that his wife had an illegitimate son!'

'I'd like to have been a fly on the wall

when he spoke to her about that!' I exclaimed. I tried to picture Ursula's reaction to the fact her secret had been discovered.

Gale waved his arm impatiently. 'The second nugget was that Ursula had been penniless and desperate for money after the birth of Peter. She'd had difficulty getting employment and had been reduced to working as a chorus-girl in a London nightclub.'

I raised my eyebrows. 'I can see why she was terrified anyone would find out about that! It would wreck her standing in any sort of decent society.'

'Much to her surprise, Bellman liked the idea of a family,' Gale continued. 'He'd lost one family, his marriage to Yvonne was childless, and here was a chance of getting another. He loved her so much he was content to overlook all that chorus-girl stuff.'

'He wanted the boy!' I cut in excitedly.

Gale nodded. 'He'd lost his two boys in the First World War. Here was a ready-made one. Bellman wanted to meet Peter, which they did two weeks ago.'

'Two weeks ago?' I was astounded. 'They visited Zoe's sister and met Peter?'

'Yes. Bellman liked the boy.'

'Bellman told you all this?'

'Last night. He unburdened himself. He knew something was badly wrong but couldn't put his finger on it.'

Suddenly it all became clear to me. Zoe's sister Lucy and her husband must have got the wind up when Ursula and Bellman turned up on her doorstep. Fearful they were going to try and take Peter from them, Lucy must have got adoption papers in a hurry. That was why Ursula wouldn't sign the adoption papers Zoe had brought with her. Everything had changed. Bellman wanted Peter to come and live with him. He'd lost his two sons thanks to the war, and wanted a male heir.

Gale was watching me intently. A huge grin spread over his face. 'You see it now, eh?'

'What about the father?' I asked.

'Ah!' Gale thumped his fist into the palm of his hand. 'That's the one fact she wouldn't tell him. She wouldn't let on who the father was because she didn't want him traced.'

'So nothing's been resolved? If the father's alive, he could have a legal claim on the boy?'

'Not if no one knows who he is. An affair that happened in Monte Carlo seven years ago — that's a while ago and a long way away.'

'Maybe Ursula doesn't know!'

Gale shook his head. 'I think she does.'

'Ursula may or may not know the real name of her son's father. But maybe . . . the birth certificate!' I exclaimed. 'We must see Peter's birth certificate. I'll speak to Zoe.'

Gale suddenly waved his arm dismissively. He had lost patience with the whole discussion. 'Let's get some breakfast, young feller,' he cried, leaping towards the door. 'I could eat a horse!'

I heard a car draw up outside, followed by a sharp knock at the front door. Gale said Ursula's doctor was expected to give her a sedative. As we crossed the hallway, I saw him climbing the stairs holding his leather bag, and assumed Zoe would come down once Ursula was asleep.

The dining room was subdued. I saw Gale march over to where Trenton was pouring the coffee and get himself a cup. Jack Merridew sat at the far end of the table looking miserable, nibbling at a piece of toast. My father waved a hand as I entered and put down the morning paper he had been reading as I went over to him.

'Terrible business, this, Jeff,' he greeted, shaking his head in sorrow. 'The worst possible outcome.'

'There's got to be an explanation.'

'I'm going to tidy up Bellman's papers as best I can and return to London. There's nothing more I can achieve by staying here. The best you can do is return with me. You've done all you can. It's a police matter; let them do their job.'

It was the perfect cue for Chief Detective Inspector Halliday and Sergeant Lockyer to enter. They looked very stern-faced. I could hear booted feet marching across the hallway and tramping up the stairs. I caught a glimpse of Jepson and Rogers with their equipment cases, followed by the police surgeon.

Then Zoe entered. She look pale, as if she hadn't slept. I crossed over to meet her. 'Good morning,' I greeted.

'There's nothing good about it. I can't believe this has happened. It's so dreadful.'

'I know. How's Ursula?'

'She was hysterical, but she's asleep now. Doctor Wyatt's given her a sedative.'

I nodded sympathetically. 'That's good.'

She gave me a despairing glance. 'None of this is good. What's going on here?'

'We'll get to the bottom of it. Somehow.'

'Excuse me,' broke in Halliday's voice. 'I'm sure you all know.' He coughed and started again, adopting more of an official approach, as the situation warranted. 'I regret to inform you Mr. Joshua Bellman has been murdered.' He paused to let this statement of fact take effect. 'My men are upstairs making their examination. While they're doing so, I would ask you to avoid going upstairs, and if possible to remain in here. No one must leave the house until we've completed our enquiries. I'll be taking statements in the front room. Each of you will be asked to give an account of the previous evening and when you last saw Mr. Bellman. Please think back and try to remember every detail. Sergeant Lockyer will call you one at a time.'

He looked over to Trenton, who was standing by the coffee jug looking mournful. 'Now, I would like to begin with you, Trenton, followed by Mrs. Jessop the cook, who I understand was the first person to discover the broken window in the scullery when she started work this morning.'

'That's correct, Inspector,' answered Trenton, looking very nervous, as if he was about to be executed.

Sergeant Lockyer could see the butler was under great strain and gave him a reassuring smile as he opened the door. 'If you'll follow me, sir,' he requested pleasantly.

Halliday and Lockyer marched out of the room, followed by a very distraught Trenton, leaving the rest of us at a loose end, not knowing what was to happen next, and feeling that we had been invaded and our freedom put at risk.

I poured myself some coffee, grabbed some toast, and sat down at the table next to Zoe. 'I expect this will take a while,' I forecast, trying to start up a casual conversation.

She sipped her coffee. 'Yes. I don't know what to say to them. I slept like a log all night. I didn't hear a thing. What am I supposed to tell them?'

'Just tell them the truth, and tell them when you last saw Bellman.'

'That was after dinner, when he went upstairs with Mr. Gale.'

'Well if that's all you can think of, just tell them that.' After a few moments I asked her in a low voice: 'Do you have Peter's birth certificate?'

She nodded. 'In my car with the adoption papers.'

'Do you know the names on it?'

She paused to remember. 'There's Ursula's name, of course.'

'What about the father?'

'It says 'father unknown'.' She saw my disappointment. 'Why — you need to know who the father is?'

'Yes, it would be very helpful.'

'I think Ursula deliberately left his name off because she didn't want to give him any rights.'

'There'd be very little chance of him being granted custody in the circumstances.'

'I know,' she said, keeping her voice low, 'but she didn't want to take that chance.'

'Is she afraid of him?'

Zoe's beautiful green eyes looked at me thoughtfully. 'Yes, I think she is.'

17

During the course of the morning, Joshua Bellman became just another dead body — the subject of police procedure and various reports. Jepson and Rogers completed their photographs of the crime scene and the break-in window in the scullery. The police surgeon completed his examination of Bellman's body. It was nearly midday by the time their work was complete and the police contingent had left the house, with the exception of Sergeant Lockyer and Chief Detective Inspector Halliday, who reconvened in the dining room.

From their analysis of the interviews, there emerged a general consensus of what had occurred. No one admitted to having heard the sound of a break-in or any disturbance from Bellman's room — they told Halliday they had heard nothing, and had been asleep.

Mrs. Jessop the cook had discovered

the broken window in the scullery when she started work that morning, and thought there had been a burglary. She mentioned the break-in to Trenton, who carried out a quick check to see if anything obvious was missing. Nothing was. He said he would inform Joshua Bellman when he took him up his morning cup of tea at seven thirty.

At first, he'd thought his master was in a deep sleep. He'd given him a gentle shake, but to no avail, and had then felt his pulse. Finding none, realised he was dead. Thinking he had died in his sleep, he'd intended to wake Ursula, but met Gale in the hallway, who had advised against waking her straight away, and examined Bellman himself. There was no evidence of murder until Gale turned him on his side and saw the knife wound. There was little blood. He had then found the card in Bellman's hand. He immediately telephoned the police.

According to the police surgeon, Joshua Bellman had been murdered in the early hours of the morning between two and three o'clock. The cause of death had been a narrow-bladed knife thrust into his back while he was sleeping, which had been withdrawn and was missing. The weapon was consistent with that used in the murders of Baker and Gifford.

Gale was standing next to Halliday, looking at us seated at the dining table like an inquisitor. 'I'd expected something like this,' he told everyone with a ferocious scowl on his face. 'Just not so soon. When I turned Joshua over, I saw the knife wound and found the card. Our sick friend had given me confirmation of what I already knew — Bellman had been visited by the Snark, and murdered like the others.'

He went over to the sideboard and poured himself a cup of coffee. He took a gulp of it, and looking round at everyone, belligerently pointing to his painting of Ursula above the fireplace. 'Small trifles,' he said, 'building up a picture, like the pieces of a jigsaw puzzle, until only one or two pieces are missing.' He gave a leering grin and stuck his chin forward. 'You see the outline around that painting — that faint black outline? That's where another painting used to be. Bellman kept it wrapped up in a blanket in a cupboard in his study. Last night he showed it to me. It was his second wife, Yvonne — so like Ursula as to be almost uncanny. It wasn't long before Ursula and Bellman were married. To celebrate, he commissioned this new painting from me.' He waved an arm in the direction of the fireplace. 'It was hung in the place of the old one, only in a slightly smaller frame, d'you see?'

We all stared at the painting of Ursula hanging above the mantelpiece, as if seeing it for the first time. It was a good likeness, having caught her pale gold hair, her porcelain features, and her finely drawn curving brows accentuating violet-blue eyes. In the painting she was wearing that same black velvet dress she'd worn to the dinner, cut low, with a single diamond clip at the breast.

Gale ran his hand through his unruly chestnut-coloured hair. 'After about a year, Bellman changed his will in her favour — a sign that everything was going well. Bellman had a weak heart, d'you see? Ursula didn't think she'd have to wait too long for nature to take its course and for her to inherit all that money.

'When Franklin Gifford first met Ursula in London, she was penniless. He realised straightaway how similar her looks were to Yvonne's, and that if he could team her up with Bellman there might be a way to regain some control over the man's empire — with Bellman becoming self-sufficient, he had lost that control, d'you see? So he wasted no time in introducing Ursula. Bellman fell for her at first sight, precisely what Gifford intended. Imagine Gifford waiting patiently like a vulture in the expectation of a share of the spoils — his commission for acting as a matchmaker!' Gale's bushy eyebrows contracted and his face contorted with disgust, making it clear to everyone in the room what he thought of Franklin Gifford, deceased.

'Why would anyone pay him any commission?' asked my father.

'Because he knew things about Ursula she didn't want known at that time: the boy Peter, performing as a chorus-girl in a London nightclub, and especially the identity of the father.'

I shifted uneasily in my chair and glanced at Zoe, who was watching Gale nervously.

'Ursula had begun an affair with a man in Monte Carlo some years before she met Bellman,' Gale explained. 'She had a child by him, now a young boy of seven. His name is Peter.'

I felt very uncomfortable at hearing this confidential information that Zoe had told me in the tearoom. She didn't know that Bellman knew and had told Gale last night, so she would think I had betrayed her confidence. I glanced again at her and saw her forehead creased in a frown. She looked dismayed.

Gale went on: 'Ursula's marriage to Bellman two years ago was the subject of an article in the *Marling Chronicle*, also one of the city financial papers, and this must have been read by the man of mystery from Monte Carlo, who then came looking for her.' He leaned forward, his beard quivering. 'And he found her!'

This was news to me. Gale hadn't told me any of this!

'He persuaded Ursula to get him a job working for Bellman. Petrified that he'd reveal her past and her illegitimate son, she agreed to cut him in on any money Bellman left her. She spoke to her husband, putting forward the argument that as he worked from home a lot more now he was married, what he needed here was an assistant, a secretary.'

This bombshell had the effect of sucking the air out of the room. Collectively everyone held their breath as they turned to look at Jack Merridew, who was staring at Gale with a face of incomprehension and almost imperceptibly shaking his head.

Gale rubbed his hands together, relishing the effect his surprise announcement had produced. 'Bellman agreed, and now we have Ursula and her former lover ensconced at Hunters Meadow, waiting for Bellman to die. That's the trouble with having too much money — people want to get their hands on it!' Gale looked again at Jack Merridew, who still wore a mask of injured injustice.

'This is n-not true,' he stuttered. 'All f-fiction.'

Gale was not in the least perturbed by this denial. 'The attraction that had brought them together in the first instance sprang back to life, and it was easy, wasn't it? Both living in the same house, they could be together whenever Bellman was away. But Ursula began to find the situation unnerving, didn't she, eh?' Gale addressed this question directly at Merridew, who said nothing. 'Of course, everyone thought Ursula was carrying on an affair with Lance Weston, which is exactly what they were supposed to think, to divert any attention from the real one. She probably teased Weston a bit, maybe even flirted with him, but I think that's about all. Village gossips filled in the rest. Because she already had a lover, d'you see?

'Bellman, despite his heart condition, seemed reasonably fit and didn't look as if he was going to pop off any time soon. Bored to death and trapped in this house, Ursula and Merridew decided their little plan needed to be accelerated, and that was when they decided to wait for the right opportunity to remove Bellman from the triangle.' Gale gave us all a Machiavellian stare as he revelled in his own cunning. 'Then things began to unravel.' He waved his arms, narrowly avoiding sending Halliday's coffee cup flying.

'Bellman became intrigued. He probably asked Ursula questions about her past and found her answers too vague. He was smart; he would've picked up on that. Her history started to rattle him, d'you see? He spoke to Franklin Gifford about her, who must have told him just enough to trigger a telephone call. Then Bellman spoke to Hilary King. He knew her husband was a private detective. He didn't tell Hilary what it was about, only that he needed someone on hand for a couple of weeks to carry out some investigative work. Robert Lawson, the man we knew as William Baker, jumped at an opportunity to be close to Hilary, in the hope of persuading her to come back and live with him. Baker met Bellman discreetly in the woods by prior arrangement, and Bellman briefed him on what he wanted done. Of course Merridew, in his role as Bellman's secretary, began to get wind that something was going on.'

Sergeant Lockyer edged towards the drawing-room door.

'Well,' Gale continued, 'the first thing Baker discovered was that Ursula had an illegitimate child. Much to her surprise, Bellman wanted to meet him, which they did two weeks ago. He liked the idea of a male heir, d'you see?' He looked directly at Zoe. 'That's why your sister Lucy and her husband suddenly came up with adoption papers and why Ursula wouldn't sign 'em, eh? Bellman wanted Peter to come and live here. Now the last thing Merridew wanted was Bellman drafting a new will leaving part to Ursula and part to Peter, or everything to Peter. We'll never know, because Bellman didn't live long enough to draft it!' Gale looked meaningfully at Merridew, who sat very still.

'Then there was the small matter of the acquisition. Bellman was going to spend a large chunk of his cash on buying out the Fisk business. Merridew could see everything slipping away. More importantly, at any moment William Baker might find out who the unknown father on Peter's birth certificate really was.' Gale uttered a strange growling noise. 'Like a fool, I gave him the very opportunity he needed to act — a burlesque; a bizarre diversion; a plan allowing him to remove permanently everyone that was in his way. A plan that was so insane it would act as a smokescreen and divert attention from his real motives.

'Baker had been in Marling; why he was there doesn't matter. He caught the last train to Farley Halt. Merridew followed him and slipped his postcard into the station post-box in time to catch the last post. I was supposed to think Baker had been killed earlier. Merridew had put his plan into action and transformed himself into the Snark! He made up his mind to kill. Alone on the platform, after the train had left, he battered Lawson over the head, and . . . well, you all know the rest.

'That leads us to Franklin Gifford. He had to be next, and quickly, because the moment Gifford heard Baker had been murdered he'd eventually put two and two together and make six. He communicated his unease to Trueman here, just before his worst fears were realised.'

Halliday looked sternly at Merridew, who looked bewildered. 'I think you'd better accompany us to the station, Mr. Merridew.'

'I d-don't understand why you would m-make this up,' Merridew replied owlishly.

'By the time I'd whittled everything down, I was left with you, Merridew,' snarled Gale. 'It took me a while to realise what was wrong. Then I realised a person is either short-sighted or long-sighted, but the same spectacles don't work for both, d'you see?'

Merridew looked at Gale as if he'd gone mad. 'I r-really d-don't understand what you're saying. I'm j-just Mr. Bellman's secretary. I have nothing to do with these murders.'

Gale laughed derisively for a few

seconds, then went very quiet and turned to Zoe. 'Miss Anderson, I wonder if you'd be kind enough to remove Mr. Merridew's spectacles.'

The room went silent with expectation.

'You're m-making a big m-mistake,' stuttered Merridew.

'Remove his spectacles, Mr. Gale?' asked Zoe nervously.

'I say, Gale,' I intervened. She plainly didn't want to be involved.

Gale ignored my protest. 'Remove his spectacles if you would be so kind, Miss Anderson,' he ordered with a frightful intensity that brooked no refusal.

Jack Merridew sat meekly while Zoe got up and took a step towards him. He obligingly looked up at her with a smile. Muttering an apology, she took off his shell-rimmed spectacles. I noticed how his eyes glittered. They didn't look meek at all.

Gale was tugging at his beard. 'Now if you would put them on.'

Zoe, anxious to get whatever it was over with as soon as possible, quickly complied. She gave a little cry. 'Why, there's no difference,' she said.

'Of course there isn't!' cried Gale. 'Because they don't do anything for near sight, or long sight, or any other kind of sight. The lenses are clear glass!'

Jack Merridew threw back his chair with incredible force as he got to his feet, owlish wisdom gone, and all pretence at meekness gone with it. 'You interfering busybody!' he snarled without a trace of a stutter, an automatic appearing in his hand.

Sergeant Lockyer stepped forward from the door.

'Stay where you are!' Merridew ordered in a harsh voice.

Whether we were all so used to Merridew appearing weak and therefore didn't consider him a sufficient threat, I don't know. I heard Sergeant Lockyer say: 'Now, put that gun down, sir.' Then a deafening report! Sergeant Lockyer staggered back, his hand at his chest, and collapsed on the floor. Halliday took a step towards him.

'Stay where you are!' ordered Merridew as he took a step sideways and turned to Zoe. 'Come here!' he barked at her. Zoe was paralysed with fear. She didn't move.

My ears were ringing and my heart was pumping so hard everyone must have heard it. I could hardly breathe, while my brain had gone into overdrive, desperately striving to provide a solution to the situation.

'Come here now or I'll shoot you in the arm!' ordered Merridew.

No one in the room doubted that he meant it. Halliday looked grim. I suspected he, too, was desperate to find a safe way out of this. Gale's face was contorted in such a fury it was terrifying to look upon.

Merridew, by contrast, looked calm and totally in charge as Zoe took a step towards him. He reached out and grabbed her by her arm so firmly that she winced.

I stood up. 'Stop that!' I cried.

'Sit down!' commanded Merridew menacingly.

I held my ground until he raised the automatic. There didn't seem much point in getting shot for nothing, so I sat down again, feeling quite useless. My heart went out to Zoe. My father's words came back to haunt me: *Occasionally, when an emotionally disturbed person feels threatened and attacked, they may think they need to retaliate — to kill before they are killed.*

'Who has the keys to the car?' snapped Merridew, looking pointedly at Halliday while lifting the barrel of the automatic a fraction of an inch.

Halliday glanced over at the still body of Sergeant Lockyer.

'Get them!' ordered Merridew.

Halliday paused. I thought he was about to refuse, and prepared myself for another shot. But he thought better of it, and glaring at Merridew, reluctantly walked over to the prone body of his sergeant. He took a bunch of keys from the dead man's jacket pocket.

Merridew had edged round the end of the table and, marching Zoe in front of him, was moving towards the door. 'Hand them out,' he instructed, 'at arm's length. Don't try anything or you'll end up like him.' He gestured with the gun at Sergeant Lockyer.

'You'll hang for this,' promised Halliday quietly, but with icy determination, as he extended his arm towards Merridew.

Merridew snatched the keys from Halliday with his left hand, never taking his eyes off anyone. He dropped them into his jacket pocket. 'Don't try to follow me or she gets it!' He kicked open the drawing-room door with his foot and pushed her roughly into the hall beyond.

We listened to their footsteps going to the front door, the sound of the lock, and the door opening and then closing. The moment Gale heard the front door close he was at the drawing-room door.

'Don't be too hasty, Mr. Gale,' warned Halliday, stepping towards him. 'Remember he's got Zoe!'

Gale, forever impetuous, leapt into the hall, turned away from the front door and instead made for the steps to the scullery. We heard car doors bang shut at the front of the house, and the engine of the police car fire up.

I was torn between prudence and

necessity. I didn't want Zoe to be in danger, but I realised if I didn't do something I might never see her again. So, casting caution to the wind, I followed Gale.

As I arrived outside the garage, Gale roared out on his thunderous orange contraption. As he went by me, he gave a leering grin.

Without thought for my safety, or my sanity, I leapt onto the pillion, and with a roar like a lion and a burst of noise like a machine gun, we gave chase.

18

The thought of Zoe sitting in the police car with Jack Merridew overruled any considerations for my own safety. The car was so far ahead it couldn't be seen, and the road snaked through high hedges, which severely cut down our visibility.

We were travelling at a dangerously lethal speed, leaning so far over when we encountered a sharp bend that I wondered how we didn't strike the surface of the road and go spinning out of control. But Gale managed to control the beast somehow. It had now warmed up and was producing its acrid blue smoke, so that anyone following us would find themselves driving into a smelly fog, though the intermittent rain that lashed my face helped keep it down.

We roared and popped, streaking past gateways and hedgerows I had previously walked past in a leisurely fashion, until we came to the green at Lower Bramsham.

The road curved round it in a semicircle before straightening towards Marling. On the far side we just glimpsed the tail of the police car.

Gale turned his head towards me. 'Hang on!' he yelled.

'I am hanging on!' I shouted back.

Then with horror I saw what he planned to do. Leaving the road, we bounced up a slope and across the grass of the green itself. I felt perilously unsafe, as if at any moment the wheels would lose their grip on the wet grass. I expected to be thrown from the pillion. Gale was leaning low over the handlebars, working the throttle like a malevolent demon, gunning every last burst of speed from his infernal machine.

I have to admit Gale's shortcut saved precious seconds, even if it took years off my life. By the time we had reached the other side of the green, we could just make out the police car streaking ahead of us on the long road to Marling. We were gradually gaining on them. But it must have been obvious to Gale that if we managed to catch up with the police car,

Merridew would see us in his rear-view mirror and might make good his threat — he might harm Zoe. The thought of such an act was intolerable. I wanted to communicate my concerns to Gale, in case his bullish desire to catch them at all costs had caused him to forget her danger, but the speed at which we were travelling prohibited any attempt at contact except digging him in the ribs.

Suddenly we rounded a bend, and along the straight road ahead the police car had disappeared. The only explanation was that they had turned off, obviously to avoid Marling, where in all likelihood Halliday had set up a road-block or they might be slowed down by other traffic. I didn't know the area well enough to predict if we were approaching a turning, or if we were, where it might lead to, and neither did Gale. We shot past a turning to our right.

Gale must have been thinking along the same lines as me, for suddenly he braked hard, skidding and throwing us forward and almost unseating me. Turning the handlebars hard left, he wrenched his horrible smoking contraption round, doubled back about twenty yards, and roared off up a single-track road full of potholes and patches of water. It was a steep climb up the side of a hill punctuated by a staccato pop-pop-pop, followed by several loud explosions. When we arrived at the summit, drenched with water and splattered with mud, and I'm sure several dislocated bones, we could see the countryside stretching out below us. About a quarter of a mile ahead was the stolen police car.

I thought of Zoe trapped with Jack Merridew, and of the macabre murders he had committed, and wished Gale could go faster, but at the same time wished he would slow down; for I feared that if we continued weaving from side to side to avoid holes in the road, we might never catch up with them at all, but end up in a ditch with this orange beast on top of us.

We shot through the small village of Crawhill, the road widening as it cut along a river valley towards Lower Fell. My face was streaked with rain, and I had to shake my head vigorously to get the water out of my eyes in order to see anything at all. Letting go of Gale would have meant certain suicide. But this inconvenience was of little consideration, as my mind was totally focused on the car ahead.

We started to climb the side of the valley, twisting and turning through woodland, so the road was obscured and we could no longer see the car ahead. Eventually the trees thinned out and we came to open moorland. I was relieved to glimpse a flash of red brake-lights telling me our quarry was still there, maintaining roughly the same distance. A signpost flashed by. We were currently headed for 'Dean Stanmoor'. Then the car ahead turned right down another minor road signposted 'Stanmoor Aeronautic Club'.

We followed, buffeted by powerful squalls as the wind gathered strength across the open terrain. A long way ahead I could make out some buildings, a small control tower and a bright red windsock that was squirming in the sudden gusts of wind. Did Merridew have access to an aircraft of some sort? The thought of Zoe being spirited away in a plane caused fear and dread to clutch at my heart. This was no weather to go flying in.

Gale suddenly turned his head and yelled something at me as he pointed furiously to a gauge. I realised he was telling me we were running out of fuel. This infernal machine was about to abandon us in the middle of nowhere!

As I saw the car ahead disappear from my view round the front of a corrugated aircraft hangar, the orange demon gave a phut-phut sound followed by a dying wheezing, like bagpipes running out of air. It looked as though we had finally run out of fuel. Gale held the clutch, and we coasted down a gentle slope to within a hundred yards of the entrance to Stanmoor Aeronautic Club. Stiff and sore, I climbed off the contraption and faced Gale.

His face was one big grin. 'Come on young feller, we're on foot from here!'

'What are we going to do?' I shouted, trying to make myself heard above a squall that blew our hair in several directions at once.

'That's a blithering idiotic question!' Gale yelled back. 'We're going to stop him!'

'He's got a gun!' I pointed out. 'And he's got Zoe!'

Gale ignored me and made off towards the airfield at a pace I struggled to keep up with. I hoped the police were not far behind us. If they did have a roadblock at Marling, they must have realised Merridew had turned off; and, knowing the area a lot better than we did, they would surely work out where. I expected to see police reinforcements at any moment.

As we approached the gate, we heard a sound I had dreaded — a nine-cylinder radial aero engine starting up. The small airfield looked deserted. I couldn't see anything until I came round the side of the hangar by the gateway. Then I saw the police car abandoned on the grass outside the hangar with its doors open. There was no sign of Zoe.

A silver biplane with a red-and-white-striped tail, its wheels stumbling over tufts of grass, was headed towards the runway. I could only see a pilot, who must have been Merridew. In a flash Zoe's words from the tearoom came back to me: *It was too late when she found out just what kind of man he was — a gambler with debts piling up, and an aviator mixed up in some shady goings-on.'* Jack Merridew was an aviator with his own plane. I was staring at it!

What had happened to Zoe?

I raced round the front of the building, my worst fears painting horrible scenes in my head, and looked inside. There were two other biplanes in the hangar. Then I saw her at the back of the building. She was handcuffed by one hand to a water pipe, looking dejected and very angry.

'Jeff!' she yelled as she saw me.

I ran frantically towards her. 'Are you hurt?' I called out.

'Never mind me!' she shouted back, struggling to free her arm to no avail.

'Where are the keys?' I asked as I reached her.

'He's got the keys with him — he's getting away!'

I don't know what I thought I could

hope to achieve against an armed man in a biplane, but I hurried out of the hangar and ran towards the craft. Merridew might have the keys to the handcuffs with him, but in his hurry to reach his plane he had obviously left the keys to the police car in the ignition. This was a huge mistake, because Gale was already in the driving seat, frantically trying to start the engine. As it screamed into life, in his impatience he was giving it too much throttle.

I could only watch helplessly as the car leapt forward, nearly stalled, then went skidding and slewing after the biplane. I could see Gale through the passenger window, his face contorted with fury, wrestling with the wheel and yelling for all he was worth. Helpless to do anything, I hurried back to Zoe, thinking that Gale was wasting his energy chasing the biplane. Merridew had got away.

Zoe was slumped against the pipe, exhausted from trying to get free. She looked up at me with an expression of frustration on her face.

'I'm sure the police will be here any

minute, and they'll have some keys,' I said soothingly.

I looked back through the opening of the hangar. The biplane was bouncing over the rough ground, still pursued by Gale in the police car. The rain and wind were so strong that they were impeding the biplane's progress. Gale was gaining; I could see the gap was closing. Every so often the wind caught a wing, lifting the plane off one set of wheels, and causing it to slew in a different direction. The rudder was waving from side to side as Merridew wrestled with the controls, attempting to stay on course towards smoother ground where he could increase his speed for take-off. At that moment the biplane was side-on to me; then it turned sharply, and I was looking at the tail and along the fuselage.

I saw Merridew's head turned towards Gale, his arm waving. There was something in his hand. Two sharp reports echoed across the airfield. I saw the windscreen of the police car shatter and Gale thrown back in the driver's seat. He'd been shot!

The car lurched from side to side a couple of times, went out of control, slewed off course, and finally stalled. Was Gale wounded or dead?

My heart sank as I ran towards the stationary police car with Gale slumped in the driving seat. I'd known all along we were ill-equipped to go chasing after an armed man, particularly such a dangerous one. This was foolhardy.

The biplane had reached smoother grass. It was gathering speed.

My eye caught a movement. I saw Gale raise his fist for a few seconds, then his arm fell, and he slumped back in the seat and was still.

A police siren sounded above the wind. A car was approaching rapidly.

I watched the biplane leave the ground.

A police car, its blue light flashing and siren screaming, sped through the gateway and onto the airfield.

It was too late! Merridew was in the air!

For a few moments the biplane hung above the ground like a great bird. Then an updraught, a tremendous squall of wind and rain, caught it under the wing and flung it sideways. The wing tip struck the ground, struts snapping. The biplane was tossed upwards and flipped over. I caught a glimpse of a frantic Merridew struggling with the controls.

The biplane crashed onto its tail, which instantly broke into matchwood. The propeller threw divots of grass into the air as the blades struck the ground. The plane slid forward, gouging out a dark groove in its wake. The cockpit windshield, ground into the earth, splintered into a thousand pieces.

I knew no one could have survived that crash.

As the stricken plane finally slewed to a halt, I saw flames spring up around the engine. There was a deafening explosion! A ball of orange fire and smoke engulfed the biplane as its full tank of fuel ignited.

I turned back to Zoe. Her mouth was open and her eyes were huge as she watched the scene in horror. The police car raced towards the wreckage.

'I'm going to Gale,' I shouted. I ran out onto the airfield and was assaulted by acrid smoke from the burning plane, as the wind changed direction for a moment and blew a black cloud of it at me.

The police car skidded to a halt. Four uniformed men whom I didn't recognise sprang out. Two of them, a sergeant and a constable, broke off immediately and ran towards the figure of Gale, still slumped in the driving seat of the stolen police car. The other two, both constables, came running towards me to cut me off.

'Stop right there, sir!' yelled one.

'It's all right,' I cried back, rain lashing my face, 'I'm with Halliday.' I pointed to the police car. 'Simon Gale was shot.' I waved my arm towards the burning biplane, which was spitting and crackling. 'Merridew shot him.'

Much to my indignation the other policeman swiftly handcuffed me. 'We'll soon sort this out, sir,' he said. 'Meanwhile, we're taking no chances.'

I realised they didn't know who was who. 'My main concern right this moment,' I said, 'is that you sort him out.' As my hands were cuffed, I could only nod my head fiercely in Gale's direction. I continued walking towards him as best I could.

A sergeant, who was bending over an unconscious Gale, turned towards me. 'He's been shot in the shoulder. Lost some blood, but I think he'll be all right.' He turned to the constable who had handcuffed me. 'Dobson, drive over to that control tower and see if you can ring for an ambulance.'

'I don't think there's time for that,' I cried. 'You need to get him into your car *now* and drive him straight to hospital! By the time an ambulance gets here, it could be too late!'

Dobson halted and looked inquiringly at his sergeant for instructions.

'You may have a point there, sir,' the sergeant conceded. 'Dobson, we'll take him.' He turned to me. 'Who is he?'

'Simon Gale,' I answered.

The sergeant turned back to Dobson. 'You take Mr. Gale to Marling General.'

'Yes, sir.'

As soon as Dobson had started the car, I nodded my head in the direction of the aircraft hangar. 'Miss Anderson is handcuffed to a pipe in there. She was held hostage. Do you have any keys? She's had a terrible time.'

The sergeant nodded. 'I'll see to it, sir.'

We both instinctively looked towards the burning plane. 'Who was in that?' asked the sergeant.

'Jack Merridew,' I answered.

'No one could survive that!' he commented gravely.

'No,' I agreed.

The sergeant rubbed his chin. 'Was he this Snark character — the one who's been committing these terrible murders?'

'Yes,' I said, 'I believe he was.'

19

Chief Detective Inspector Halliday eventually arrived at the airfield. The death of his sergeant obviously weighed terribly upon him, and Simon Gale getting himself shot only added to his troubles. He looked drawn, his cheerful countenance had disappeared, and he seemed to have aged ten years. When he saw me handcuffed, he apologised profusely and ordered one of the constables to remove the cuffs immediately.

'They didn't know who Merridew was, that was their problem,' he explained. 'Come to think of it, we still don't know who Merridew *really* was, do we?'

'No,' I admitted.

Halliday was frowning. 'Have I missed something, Mr. Trueman? How did Mr. Gale know that the Snark was Jack Merridew?'

I laughed. 'An intelligent bluff, I'd say, that paid off!'

'I'd never have been able to pull off a stunt like that. Totally against all regulations.'

'That's where Gale has the advantage. I don't think he takes much notice of them.'

Halliday smiled. 'I think you're right there,' he agreed. 'What happened here? How did Mr. Gale get shot?'

I rapidly explained to Halliday what had happened from the time I had arrived at the airfield to the moment when Constable Dobson drove Gale off to Marling General. When I had finished, he shook his head.

'Mr. Gale shouldn't play the hero,' he said grimly. 'He could easily have got himself killed, if he hasn't already. I hope he pulls through.'

The flames that had engulfed the biplane had died down, and now all that remained was a skeleton of what had once been a fine aircraft and somewhere within the glowing embers another skeleton, the charred bones of Jack Merridew.

Zoe and I sat quietly in the back of the police car as we were driven to Marling

Police Station. We had plenty to occupy our thoughts. It was gone three o'clock in the afternoon when we arrived in Marling, and gone seven in the evening by the time we'd completed our statements and left the police station. Sometime between arrival and departure, Ursula Bellman had been arrested.

Zoe took my arm and looked up at me in that wonderful way of hers. 'I'm going to take you to dinner,' she said in her husky, attractive voice. 'I think you deserve it after rescuing a damsel in distress!'

'It's I who should take you for dinner,' I protested. 'I didn't rescue you at all!'

'Well you almost did,' she said, squeezing my arm. 'I was abandoned, handcuffed to a water pipe, and you consoled me until the keys arrived.'

I looked at my mud-spattered trousers. They had dried out with awful creases, and bagged at the knees. 'They won't let me in anywhere like this!' I protested.

'I'm sure it'll be all right.' She laughed. 'Your trousers are a minor problem compared to what we've just been through!' She frowned and gave a huge sigh. 'What a truly dreadful morning!'

'We have a right to enjoy ourselves after such a morning,' I assured her. 'But first, do you know where Marling General Hospital is? I'd like to call in and see how Simon Gale's getting on.'

We learned that he was in intensive care and unable to receive visitors, but that he was in a stable condition and we ought to be able to visit him tomorrow.

We found a small restaurant close by and chose a table tucked away in a dimly lit corner, where my dishevelled appearance wouldn't be so obvious to other diners. We both had chicken and mushroom vol-au-vents with a butter and wine sauce, accompanied by a bottle of Chablis.

'This is delicious!' Zoe popped another piece of vol-au-vent into her mouth. She looked at me, her impish face broke into a warm smile, and those dimples . . . She was not just referring to the taste of the food when she said: 'I'm really enjoying this.'

'So am I!' I squeezed her hand briefly.

'I hope nothing else happens today to spoil it.'

She nodded. 'I have to ask — what do you think will happen to Ursula?'

'She's been arrested as an accessory after the fact. She may not have actually taken part in any of the murders, but she colluded in them by not going to the police and telling them what she knew.'

Zoe winced. 'Do you think they'll be able to prove that?'

'It depends what evidence they can find. You've known Ursula a lot longer than I have. Do you think she's capable of cold-blooded murder?'

Zoe sat back in her chair and breathed out slowly. 'No, I don't. She's stupid, but not wilfully evil like Jack Merridew. She likes the power money can provide, and she's foolish as I told you, but cold-blooded . . . '

'She must've known what Merridew was doing. After all, he wouldn't have got anything out of Bellman's death except through her.' Bellman's death? It was hard to think that only a short while ago I was in his office working with him on his acquisition, and now he was gone.

Zoe looked at me defensively. 'I think she was prepared to wait. That wretched man obviously wasn't.'

I took a sip of wine. 'I'd like to know more about him — about his past.' I smiled apologetically. 'Gale's turned me into a bloodhound. It's hard to give up the scent.'

I looked at my watch. I could have sat all night talking to her in that restaurant, but it was getting late and we needed transport.

She read my mind. 'Shall we have coffee and then get back to Hunter's Meadow?' she suggested.

'We'll have to get a car.'

'Well, I'm not getting the train to Farley Halt!' she said. 'You can rule that out!'

'We couldn't if we wanted to. The last train left ages ago.' I called the waiter over and asked him if he could arrange a car.

Zoe ordered coffee and then turned to me. 'Once we get back, I'm packing and returning to London in the morning. With Ursula under arrest and Mr.

Bellman gone, who will look after Hunter's Meadow?'

I was dismayed at hearing Zoe was packing and returning to London. It was all I could do not to let my disappointment show on my face. 'I expect my father's asked Trenton to stay on, at least until things are sorted out.'

I hadn't thought about leaving. I would also have to get back, and so would my father. He'd be anxious to get back to his London office to manage Bellman's affairs and other duties.

'I can give you a lift if you like,' Zoe offered.

I leapt at the opportunity to spend more time in her company. 'I'd like that very much.'

'Where do you live?'

'I have a flat in Bloomsbury.'

She hesitated. 'Do you live on your own?'

'Yes. I like to be independent. My parents have a house in Highgate.'

'My aunt left me a house in Chelsea, Markham Square. It needs renovating, but when it's all done I think it'll be quite nice.' She gave me a tap on the arm. 'You must visit and tell me what you think of the house. I'd value your opinion. I quite often go to The Pheasantry Club. It's just down the road; actors and artists go there. It has a restaurant and bar. Perhaps we could go there for a glass of wine, and catch up.'

'I'd like that very much.'

★   ★   ★

The following morning, Hunter's Meadow felt strange and empty, like we'd travelled in time. There were three of us in the dining room: myself, my father and Zoe. Trenton managed to provide coffee, toast and boiled eggs for breakfast. Mrs. Jessop had left, so there was no hot food. Trenton looked worn out and defeated, his routine permanently disrupted. He was obviously very worried for his future. I mentioned this concern to my father, who smiled. 'Don't worry, Bellman left him well provided for in his will.'

Soon we set about leaving. There were boxes of deeds, accounts, and other paperwork connected with the acquisition that had to go with my father back to our London office. 'I've arranged to take the Rolls,' he said. 'I'll return it when I come down for the inquest.'

I chose a moment when Zoe and I were alone. 'I have a request,' I began tentatively.

'Of course we'll visit Simon Gale before we go up to London,' she answered with a grin. 'I intend to get him some flowers.'

I didn't think Gale would be very interested in a bunch of cut flowers, but I didn't say anything, because Zoe had given me an idea. 'Could we stop off at Lance Weston's on the way?' I asked apologetically.

Zoe wasn't quite so enthusiastic. 'Why do you need to see him?' she asked, frowning.

'You'll find out,' I answered mysteriously.

★ ★ ★

Gale lay propped up in his hospital bed, his left shoulder swathed in bandages, looking thoroughly bad-tempered as Zoe and I walked in.

'You have visitors,' said Nurse Gregory, by now used to his tantrums, and who treated him like her six-year-old son. 'Sit up and try to behave!'

'I hope we're not disturbing you,' I said, coming fully into the room carrying a shopping bag. 'I'm sure you need as much rest — '

'I don't need any rest at all!' snapped Gale, and upon seeing Zoe he cocked an eyebrow and gave me a cheeky look.

'Now, Mr. Gale!' warned Nurse Gregory, giving him the evil eye. 'We'll have none of that!'

Gale made a face at her. He turned to us and indicated two chairs with his good arm. 'Please sit down,' he invited, glaring at Nurse Gregory's behind as she left the room. 'Good God almighty, that woman is not human! She took my tobacco!' he growled.

'I thought you might like these.' Zoe held up a bunch of yellow chrysanthemums we had just bought.

Gale eyed the flowers suspiciously. I

could see he couldn't care less about them.

'Can I put them in this?' she asked, indicating an empty glass vase on the bedside table.

Gale grunted affirmatively.

Zoe went over to a wash basin, filled the vase with water, and arranged the flowers delicately. Then she put the vase back on the bedside table and surveyed her handiwork. 'There we are! That's brightened the place up!'

Gale grunted again.

'Now, I'll leave you two to have a chat while I go and have a cup of tea,' she said tactfully, giving me a meaningful look.

Once she had left the room, I delved into my bag and produced two packs. 'I've brought you some marshmallows,' I said with a reassuring grin.

'Marshmallows!' Gale's face contorted into something representing a gargoyle. 'What good are marshmallows?'

'Well — '

'What I need,' he insisted ungratefully, 'is to escape from this torture chamber and get my hands on a tankard of beer!'

'Ah!' I had got the result I was looking for, but couldn't resist teasing him some more. 'Marshmallows are very good for packing,' I told him.

'That's about all they're good for,' he grumbled ungratefully.

I delved into my bag again, then held up a quart bottle of Lance Weston's homemade brew. The transformation of Gale's features was a sight to behold. It was like the sun bursting through storm clouds. The scowl on his face evaporated completely, to be replaced by a huge grin.

'By Jove! Trueman, you've brought home the bacon!' He tried to sit up and I saw him wince with pain. His eyes darted around the small hospital room and fixed on the vase of yellow chrysanthemums. 'Throw those away, quick!' he snapped. 'Chuck 'em in the sink!'

I was about to protest; then, remembering I was dealing with Simon Gale, I laughed, did as I was bid, and held up the empty vase like a trophy.

'It should hold nearly two pints!' he cried optimistically as I emptied the entire contents of the bottle, gently so as not to create a froth, into the glass vase. He took it from me, wincing again as his shoulder felt the action, and swallowed a prodigious draft.

'That was good!' he said, having emptied half of it. Then his face suddenly fell and he looked guilty. 'Did you want some?' he asked.

I shook my head, producing a second bottle. I reached for his more modest-sized water glass for my own share, before topping him up. His huge grin returned.

I delved into my bag again. 'I thought you might like this to read,' I said, holding up the autumn number of *The Motorcycle Magazine*.

'Aha!' cried Gale, feasting his eyes on the cover. 'You know, young feller, you've turned out quite well!'

20

It was three weeks since Jack Merridew had met his demise after shooting Simon Gale, and Ursula Bellman had been arrested as an accessory after the fact, when I received an invitation to come to lunch at Gale's house in Ferncross. He had scribbled across the bottom: 'Bring Zoe along.' I telephoned her and she said she'd love to come. I followed a road map, issuing directions while she drove. It was a chilly October day, but the sky was clear, and it was lovely weather for a drive to the country.

Gale's house was hidden behind a very high and straggly hedge. It took us a few minutes to find the gate. We followed a short path through thick shrubbery, wondering what to expect. We came to a long, low house in the shape of an L, against a backdrop of tall trees and open countryside.

As we approached the door, looking for

a knocker or a bell, or some means of announcing our presence, it opened as if by magic, and Simon Gale's larger-than-life presence filled the threshold. He was dressed in the most extraordinary outfit of lime-green and purple tartan trousers with an orange threadbare sweater.

'Hello, hello!' he boomed, with a huge grin.

'How did you know we were here?' I asked. 'There's no bell.'

'The step, d'you see?' cried Gale enthusiastically, pointing to the large stone slab we were standing on. 'Any weight on the step triggers a bell in the kitchen, and in the evening, my studio. Now come in! Come in!' He led the way through a square hall, with odds and ends stuffed in glass cases and on shelves, into an enormous room that obviously occupied the longer arm of the house. It was a combination of living area and workshop that only a confirmed bachelor would have occupied.

Immediately to my left was an open door that I could see led into a spacious kitchen. Along from this door was a great open fireplace of red brick with a stack of logs beside it, and several huge comfortable-looking armchairs scattered in front of it. There were books and magazines everywhere, crammed into shelves that had obviously been built wherever there was a vacant wall space, and piled in heaps on the floor and on several tables. Further along the same wall was a long bench littered with all kinds of debris, and with a glue-pot in a tin saucepan standing on a gas ring, and a motorcycle exhaust pipe. Above the bench was a long rack stuffed with tools of every sort and description.

At the far end of the room, in front of a large window, was an artist's area. It was dominated by a big studio-easel next to an old dinner wagon on rubber wheels laden with jars of brushes, tubes of paint, palettes, and all the paraphernalia of a painter. I caught the faint smell of turpentine and linseed oil in the air. Against the nearby wall was stacked a pile of canvases of all sizes and shapes. I thought of Ursula's portrait and assumed this was where it had been painted.

Dividing the painting and work area off from the rest of the room was an enormous desk that faced three more windows, through which I caught a glimpse of fruit trees and flowerbeds. There were a typewriter and a telephone on the desk, which was piled with books and papers, and in front of which stood a swivel-chair. The whole place was incredibly untidy, but it was an untidiness that gave an impression of comfort.

Gale gave Zoe an appraising glance. 'Sit down, my dear,' he said. 'How have you been keeping? Have you seen a lot of this young feller here?' He slapped me on the back, and I had to re-balance myself quickly to avoid falling over.

Zoe blushed. 'I suppose we have seen each other a bit.'

'Good! That's very good! Now, to really important things. Let me get you weary travellers something to drink.' He looked first at Zoe. 'Whisky and ginger?'

'You remembered!' she said.

He roared with laughter. 'I may have been shot, but I'm not senile!' He searched for some whisky amongst a cluster of bottles and poured out a generous amount, added some ginger ale, and handed it to her. 'One happy customer!' he chortled.

'How's the shoulder?' I asked.

'A bit stiff, needs oiling, but could've been worse.'

'You could've been killed,' said Zoe.

'But I wasn't!' He switched his attention to me. 'And we'll have some beer, eh?' He snatched two tankards from a shelf containing a collection of pewter tankards and old German drinking mugs.

I was feeling very thirsty after our trip. 'Some beer would be very welcome,' I replied.

While Gale disappeared into the kitchen, I stood before the roaring fire and admired Zoe with a grin. She grinned back, shaking her head with disbelief at the general appearance and eccentricity of our host. Reaching forward, she looked humorously into my eyes as she touched my hand. 'This is fun,' she whispered.

I raised my eyebrows and grinned. 'Don't speak too soon!' I retorted in a low voice. I could hear Gale banging about in the kitchen.

She opened her green eyes wide. 'I wonder what we're going to get for lunch.'

'Simon Gale is the inventor of Gale's Golden Flakes. Perhaps we'll get a large bowl of them!'

Gale burst back into the room carrying two foaming tankards and proudly handed me one. 'There you are, young feller. See how you like that!'

I took a draft of very agreeable ale. 'That's very good!'

'It's local, d'you see? The real stuff! It's nice to see you two again!' he cried, then cocked one eyebrow. 'When are you getting married?'

We both simultaneously burst out laughing. 'We've haven't even become engaged!' I blurted out, feeling my face flush red. I saw Zoe didn't know how to respond either. If Gale had wanted to embarrass us, he had succeeded, but he didn't seem to be aware of the effect he'd had.

He looked astounded. 'Not engaged!'

he cried, stepping back in mock amazement. 'You must remedy that immediately!' He grabbed Zoe's hand and scrutinised her ring finger. Seeing no ring, he shook his head in disappointment. 'It's quite obvious to me that you ought to be!' He drank the remains of his beer, waved a big arm impatiently, and threw a huge log onto the fire. 'Come, bring your drinks into the kitchen, and let's eat!'

The kitchen was spacious, with a Swedish Aga, a number of pots and pans hanging from a ceiling frame, a free-standing beechwork surface that looked to be about four inches thick, and, at the window end, overlooking the garden, a large scrubbed farmhouse table laid for three. In a corner, by an outside door and washroom, a pin of beer rested on a trestle. It was a warm and friendly room.

'Sit yourselves down while I get this ready.' He grabbed a bottle of red burgundy, which he had already opened, and banged it down on the table. 'Help yourselves to that,' he ordered. Crossing over to the pin on its trestle and turning on a tap, he refilled his tankard. 'I'll stick with beer.'

I poured us out some wine and we watched, entranced, as he busied himself very efficiently with an assortment of vegetables, neatly putting them all in a large serving dish. Then he opened one of the Aga's heavy cast-iron doors and took out a roast suckling pig that filled the kitchen with the most appetising smell.

'That looks wonderful!' said Zoe in anticipation. 'Do you like cooking?'

'Of course I do. I like most things, Miss Anderson, particularly inventing new things to eat — or even reinventing old things!' He placed the roast suckling pig on the table. 'Easiest thing in the world to cook — five hours in the oven and there we are! Now, I hope you're hungry!'

Gale carved us succulent slices of pork. The meat was pale and tender and the skin crisp and delicious, and for a while we were so busy eating we didn't say much. Then Gale took a draft of his beer and, slamming down the tankard, asked Zoe: 'Have you been in touch with Ursula?'

'Yes,' she replied. 'She's out on bail and back at Hunter's Meadow. She signed the custody papers for Peter. I think she realised it was a burden she didn't want.'

'More like couldn't cope with,' grunted Gale disapprovingly. 'How was she?'

'She seemed very distant and cold. She's a bag of nerves, waiting to see if they prosecute.'

'Ah!' cried Gale. 'Yes, I bet she's squirming.'

'Do you think they will?' I asked. 'It's hard to believe she didn't know Merridew killed those people.' I looked at Gale's shoulder and added, 'Nearly killed you.'

He nodded. 'But you have to prove intent, d'you see? If she unwittingly helped a criminal by getting him a job, that's not exactly being an accessory to murder.'

'Of course she knew who Merridew really was,' I retorted, 'and we know he was a con man who was only there to get a share of Bellman's money, and was eager for his death.'

Gale nodded. 'But did she know he was capable of committing murder? Did she unwittingly get him a place in that house for other reasons, as she insists?'

What other reasons?' asked Zoe.

'To continue his role as her lover,' I jumped in, 'under the same roof!'

'He was genuinely employed by Bellman as his secretary, albeit at Ursula's suggestion,' answered Gale. 'She's not committed a crime by getting him a job, however unethical the whole situation was.'

'How can it ever be proved that she persuaded Merridew to bump off Bellman?' I asked. 'I thought it was his idea because he got impatient waiting for Bellman to die. Keeping up that pretence must've been quite a strain on him.'

Gale grunted, stuffing a huge forkful of crackling into his mouth. He chewed this for a few moments, making a dreadful noise, obviously formulating a reply. 'We can guess, but we can't prove it. She admits she got him the position, but will only admit he was there as a friend, and of course the father of her child, to support her in a difficult time. She won't admit he was there as her lover. She also refuses to accept she married Bellman for his money. She insists she had no idea Merridew committed the murders. She insists she assumed the murders were the actions of a lunatic.' Gale threw up his hands. 'Many others thought so too, including the police, so she was on firm ground there — exactly what the Snark wanted everyone to believe!'

'So there's nothing to link her to the murders,' I said.

'Then there won't be any prosecution?' asked Zoe, looking relieved.

'At worst, a summary offence,' I volunteered. 'She has no previous criminal history, does she?'

Zoe pursed her lips. 'I don't think so.'

'Well then,' I continued, 'if they can't get positive proof, I doubt any prosecution will get very far.'

'We'll just have to wait and see,' answered Gale. 'No prosecution doesn't mean she's not guilty, eh? As guilty as sin!'

I wondered if anything more had been discovered about Merridew. 'Was Jack Merridew his real name?'

'No,' answered Gale. 'He'd invented that name for Hunter's Meadow. Halliday turned up his real name: Jack Mervyn Duikas.'

I could see how that might morph into Jack Merridew. 'What about Franklin Gifford?' I asked, diverting the subject from Ursula, as I could see it was upsetting Zoe.

'The dead can't speak!' cried Gale.

I pursued my diversionary path. 'How's Hilary? I suppose I should call her Mrs. Lawson.'

'Agnes Beaver told me that Hilary was her niece. That's why she came to live in Lower Bramsham after that chap Ross King died. She could've stayed with her, but wanted her independence, so Miss Beaver found her the cottage. She was very cut up when this Ross chap died suddenly, and wanted to be near someone who loved her.'

'Until she met Franklin Gifford,' I murmured. 'Poor Hilary lost both the men in her life in the space of a few days.'

'Did you hear that she tried to take her own life?' Gale asked.

We shook our heads.

'After the police dropped her off home that day they took her in for questioning, she swallowed some pills. Fortunately Miss Beaver went round to see her about something. She saved her just in time.'

'That's terrible,' said Zoe. 'This has just been the most dreadful business.'

Gale followed his roast suckling pig with a delectable chocolate pudding. When we had finished, he insisted we go back into the other room, and asked Zoe to sit for him while he made preliminary sketches for a portrait.

'He's really a very nice man, isn't he?' she whispered to me when he was out of earshot.

I nodded. 'Underneath all that bluster and lunacy.'

Gale placed a canvas on the studio-easel and worked feverishly with a soft pencil, totally absorbed in transferring Zoe's likeness to the white canvas surface. After a while he stopped, leaned back, raised one eyebrow and rubbed his hands together with satisfaction. 'That should crack it,' he said. 'I'll have it finished in a couple of weeks for you.'

I saw that Zoe was about to protest.

'Hell's bells,' he cried, 'can't a feller give you a decent engagement present?'

Epilogue

A year almost to the day following our lunch with Simon Gale, Zoe and I were married in Chelsea. The charges against Ursula Bellman were eventually dropped due to lack of evidence. Fourteen months from the death of Joshua Bellman, Ursula inherited her husband's estate and became a very wealthy widow. She went to live in Knightsbridge. Hunter's Meadow was sold. Trenton received sufficient money from Bellman's estate to buy himself a small cottage in Lower Bramsham.

Ursula was frequently spotted at the most exclusive restaurants and clubs in London. Following the coronation of George VI in May 1937, Ursula was seen at several royal events marking the occasion, and it was at one of these that she met Duke Friedrich Wilhelm von Strasser of Lieben. I read in the papers they were married at the Cathedral of Cologne in November that same year, a very grand affair to which Zoe and I were invited. We declined.

Following a short stay at von Strasser's castle, the Schloss Lieben on the Rhine, Ursula and her duke travelled from Cologne to London on an airliner owned by the Belgian airline Sabena. The flight was scheduled to stop at Brussels, but the weather was so bad the pilot was forced to continue to Ostend, where conditions were little better. While circling to land at Stene Airport, the tip of a wing hit a factory chimney, ripping away the wing and an engine. The airliner burst into flames and plummeted to the ground, killing all passengers and crew.

GRIM DEATH
MURDER IN MANUSCRIPT
THE GLASS ARROW
THE THIRD KEY
THE ROYAL FLUSH MURDERS
THE SQUEALER
MR. WHIPPLE EXPLAINS
THE SEVEN CLUES
THE CHAINED MAN
THE HOUSE OF THE GOAT
THE FOOTBALL POOL MURDERS
THE HAND OF FEAR
SORCERER'S HOUSE
THE HANGMAN
THE CON MAN
MISTER BIG
THE JOCKEY
THE SILVER HORSESHOE
THE TUDOR GARDEN MYSTERY
THE SHOW MUST GO ON
SINISTER HOUSE
THE WITCHES' MOON
ALIAS THE GHOST
THE LADY OF DOOM
THE BLACK HUNCHBACK

THE WHISPERING WOMAN

Gerald Verner

Paula Rivers, a beautiful, haughty young cinema cashier, is selling tickets when her sister Eileen delivers a portentous note to her: *'Be careful. People who play with fire get badly burned. Sometimes they die.'* Not long afterward, Paula is found murdered in her booth, shot from behind. Who was the haggard old woman dressed in black who had accosted Eileen and told her to give Paula the note? Called to investigate, Superintendent Budd is faced with one of the most curious mysteries of his career.